HOLD ON TO THE SUN

OTHER BOOKS IN THE REUBEN/RIFKIN SERIES

Arguing with the Storm: Stories by Yiddish Women Writers
edited by Rhea Tregbov

Dearest Anne: A Tale of Impossible Love
by Judith Katzir

Dream Homes: From Cairo to Katrina, an Exile's Journey
by Joyce Zonana

Shalom India Housing Society
by Esther David

If a Tree Falls: A Family's Quest to Hear and Be Heard
by Jennifer Rosner

The Reuben/Rifkin Jewish Women Writers Series
A joint project of the Hadassah-Brandeis Institute
and the Feminist Press

Series editors: Elaine Reuben, Shulamit Reinharz, Gloria Jacobs

The Reuben/Rifkin Jewish Women Writers Series, established in 2006 by Elaine Reuben, honors her parents, Albert G. and Sara I. Reuben. It remembers her grandparents, Susie Green and Harry Reuben, Bessie Goldberg and David Rifkin, known to their parents by Yiddish names, and recalls family on several continents, many of whose names and particular stories are now lost. Literary works in this series, embodying and connecting varieties of Jewish experiences, will speak for them, as well, in the years to come.

Founded in 1997, the Hadassah-Brandeis Institute (HBI), whose generous grants also sponsor this series, develops fresh ways of thinking about Jews and gender worldwide by producing and promoting scholarly research and artistic projects. Brandeis professors Shulamit Reinharz and Sylvia Barack Fishman are the founding director and codirector, respectively, of HBI.

HOLD ON TO THE SUN
True Stories and Tales

MICHAL GOVRIN
Edited by Judith G. Miller

THE
FEMINIST PRESS
AT THE CITY UNIVERSITY
OF NEW YORK
NEW YORK CITY

Published in 2010 by the Feminist Press
at the City University of New York
The Graduate Center
365 Fifth Avenue, Suite 5406
New York, NY 10016

feministpress.org

First printing, October 2010

Cover design by Faith Hutchinson
Text design by Drew Stevens

State of the Arts

NYSCA

This publication was made possible, in part, by public funds from
the New York State Council on the Arts, a state agency.

Library of Congress Cataloging-in-Publication Data

Govrin, Michal, 1950-
   [Le-ehoz ba-shemesh. English]
   Hold onto the sun : true stories and tales / by Michal Govrin ; edited
and revised translations by Judith G. Miller. — 1st Feminist Press ed.
       p. cm.
   ISBN 978-1-55861-673-8 (alk. paper)
   I. Miller, Judith, 1947- II. Title.
   PJ5054.G665L413 2010
   892.4'36—dc22

                                                            2010024283

For Haim

The book before us, which gathers together fiction, poetry, and essays, is a work of art of the highest quality. The theme ranging across the entire volume is the indelible mark left by the Second World War and the Holocaust.

Michal Govrin was born in Israel, but her mother's family, including her first husband and their son, were murdered in the Holocaust. Surviving, she transmitted to her daughter not only the horror of the times, but also the strength and courage needed in saving lives during the war, and in its aftermath.

This work joins the few serious books that try through artistic means to face the unspeakable.

— Aharon Appelfeld

CONTENTS

WON'T YOU SEE

Won't you see that I am carried to you on a sea of death
Not on the Styx—that noble river in a marble inferno
No Charon poles the raft
On my cheeks still lie the curls of the brother
In whose death I live
His breath is the wind in my hair

Won't you hear, in our throats' echoes, the silence
The cry that does not relent, does not release—
Of the heads
From whose number a hand was left
To knead our lives

Won't you see
Lining up behind our faces
The trains that have carried us
On a journey ordained from then and there
Their whistle is our canopy
A pillar of smoke leading us
To the far ends of the wind

THE JOURNEY TO POLAND

(ESSAY)

PART I: A RETROSPECTIVE
NOTE FROM JERUSALEM, 1997

In late October 1975, when I was in my early twenties and completing my doctorate in Paris, I went to Poland. An almost impossible journey then for a young woman, alone, with an Israeli passport, at the time when there were no diplomatic relations between the Eastern Bloc and Israel. It was only because of a French-Jewish friend, who turned me into a "representative of France" at the International Theater Festival in Wroclaw [Breslau], that I received a special visa for a week.

The night before the trip, when everything was ready, I called my parents in Tel Aviv and told them. I asked my shocked mother for the exact address of her family home in Krakow. Only later that winter, when I visited Israel, did I understand what profound emotion took hold of my mother's few surviving friends and relatives from Krakow when they heard of the trip.

A week later I returned to Paris. For twenty-four hours, I closed myself in my student apartment in the Latin Quarter, far from the Parisian street scenes, and feverishly wrote to my parents. A letter of more than twenty pages. First thoughts, a summary of the rapid notes taken on the trip. The words groped for another language, for a different level of discourse.

That year, as every year, a commemoration for the Jewish community of Krakow was held in the auditorium of my high school in Tel Aviv. News of my trip and of my letter reached the members of the community, and they wanted to read it aloud at the commemoration. I agreed, and after it was commandeered from the family circle, I submitted it for publication to the literary supplement of the newspaper, *Davar*, with the title, "Letter from The Regions of Delusion," the expression "Regions of Delusion" borrowed from the title of a parable attributed to the Ba'al Shem Tov.* Aside from some peripheral changes of style, that text appears in the following pages.

Traveling to Poland in 75 was not part of the social phenomenon it is today. The group definition of "second-generation Holocaust survivors" hadn't yet been coined. You had to find out everything by yourself: how to plan the trip, how to feel, and how to talk about it. The letter to my par-

* (1700–60) Charismatic founder and first leader of Hasidism in Eastern Europe.

ents began a long process of formulation. Even the choice of parents as the addressees of an intimate discourse was not the norm then.

Today, that trip seems like a geological rift that changed my emotional and intellectual landscape, and placed its seal on my writing. Yet the "journey to Poland" didn't begin in 75, but in early childhood, in Tel Aviv in the 1950s. Distant shocks preceded the rift.

The "journey to Poland" began in that journey "to there"— the journey every child makes to the regions before she was born, to the unknown past of her parents, to the secret of her birth. My journey to Mother's world began long before I "understood" who my mother, Regina-Rina Poser-Laub-Govrin, was, before I "knew" that she survived the "Holocaust," that she once had another husband, that I had a half-brother. But there was the other "knowledge," that knowledge of pre-knowledge and of pre-language, transmitted in the thousand languages that connect a child and her parents without words. A knowledge that lay like a dark cloud on the horizon. Terrifying and seductive.

For years the journey proceeded on a double track. One outside the home and one inside it. And there was an almost complete separation between the two. As if everything that was said outside had nothing to do with Mother. Outside, incomprehensible, violent stories about the "Holocaust" were forged upon the little girl's consciousness. In school assemblies, in lessons for Holocaust Memorial Day, and later on in lessons of "Annals of the Jewish People," which were taught separately from "history" classes, and described events that happened in "another, Jewish time and place," where King David and small-town Jews strolled among the goats and railroad cars of the ghetto. Even the Eichmann trial, on the radio in school and at home, was an event you had to listen to, but it had no real relation to Mother. (And even if things were said about it then at home, I succeeded in repressing them from consciousness.)

At home, there were bright stories about Krakow, the boulevards, the Hebrew high school, the cook, the maids, about skiing and summer holidays in the mountains, in Zakopane, and sometimes on Friday evening, Mother and I would dance a Krakowiak* on the big rug in the living room. And there was Mother's compulsive forced-labor house cleaning, and her periods of rage and despair when I didn't straighten up my room (what I called "prophecies of rage" with self-defensive cunning), there was the everlasting, frightened struggle to make me eat, and there was the disconnected silence that enveloped her when she didn't get out of bed on Yom Kippur. And there was the photo album "from there" at the bottom of Mother's lingerie drawer, with unfamiliar images, and also pictures of a boy, Marek. And stories about him, joyful, a baby in a cradle on the balcony,

* A lively Polish dance from the Krakow region.

a beautiful child on the boulevard. And a tender memory of the *goggle-moggle** with sugar he loved so much (and only years later did I understand the terrifying circumstances of that). And there were the weekly get-togethers at Aunt Tonka's house (who was never introduced as the widow of Mother's older brother who was murdered), get-togethers so different from the humorous, confident gatherings of Father's family, who immigrated as pioneers in the 1920s and held leadership positions in the establishment of the state. At night, in Aunt Tonka's modest apartment, I was the only little girl—"a blonde, she looks like a shiksa"—in the middle of the Polish conversation of "friends from there." And every year there were also the visits of Schindler, when you could go all dressed up with Mother's cousin to greet him at the Dan Hotel. And once, when Mother and I were coming back from downtown on bus number 22, Mother stopped next to the driver and blurted a short sentence at him for no reason. The driver, a gray-haired man in a jacket, was silent and turned his head away. "He was a *ka-po*,"† she said when we got off, pronouncing the pair of incomprehensible syllables gravely. All of that was part of the cloud that darkened the horizon, yes, but had nothing to do with what was mentioned at school or on the radio.

---

* A drink of raw egg mixed into milk, in this case probably a stolen egg mixed with some sugar.

† (German) A *kapo* was a privileged prisoner of the Nazi concentration camps who served as a supervisor of the barracks.

Poland and Krakow weren't "real" places either, no more than King Solomon's Temple, for instance. I remember how stunned I was when I went with Mother to the film *King Matthew the First*, based on the children's story by Janusz Korszak which I had read in Hebrew. In the film, the children spoke Polish! And it didn't sound like the language of the friends at Aunt Tonka's house. "Nice Polish," Mother explained, "of Poles." Poles? They apparently do exist somewhere.

Yet, a few events did form a first bridge between the outside and inside. One day, in a used bookstore in south Tel Aviv, Mother bought an album of black and white photos of Krakow; "Because the photos are beautiful," she emphasized, "they have artistic value." And indeed, the sights of the renaissance city in four seasons flowed before my eyes. A beautiful, tranquil city, full of green trees and towers. Jews? No, there were no Jews in that album, maybe only a few alleys "on the way to Kazimierz."

At the age of ten, my parents sent me for private lessons in English, because "it's important to know languages." And thus I came to Mrs. Spiro, a gentle woman from London, married to Doctor Spiro, Mother's classmate from the Hebrew high school in Krakow. One day, when the lesson was over, Mrs. Spiro accompanied me to the edge of the yard of their house on King Solomon Street. I recall the sidewalk with big paving stones as she talked with me. Maybe I had complained before about Mother's strict demands, or maybe she started talking on her own.

"Of course, you know what your mother went through, she was in the Holocaust. You have to understand her, the tensions she has sometimes," she said to me directly.

That was an earthquake. A double one. The understanding that Mother was in "the Holocaust," that awful thing they talk about in school assemblies, with the "six million." And that I, a ten-year-old girl, had to or even could "understand Mother." That is, to leave the symbiosis of mother and daughter constituting one expanded body, to cut myself off from my child's view, and see Mother as a separate person, with her own fate and reasons for moods that didn't depend only on me, or on my certain guilt. I remember how, at that moment, facing the spotted paving stones, I understood both those things all at once. Like a blinding blow.

Then came high school in Tel Aviv. Since both the principal and the assistant principal were graduates of the Hebrew High School in Krakow, their former classmates in that high school, including my mother, sent their children to study there. At that school, influenced by the principal and his assistant, both of them historians, there was an intense awareness of the Jewish past and life in the Diaspora—a rare dimension in the Zionist-Israeli landscape of Diaspora denial—and Gideon Hausner, the prosecutor in the Eichmann trial, initiated a "club to immortalize the Jewish community of Krakow." A group of students met with members of the Krakow community, who taught them the history of the city and the Jewish community before the destruction. The club also heard testimony from the Holocaust, with a special (exclusive?) emphasis on the activities of the Jewish underground. The women's revolt in the Gestapo prison, led by "Justina,"* was also dramatized and performed for the community members on the annual memorial day. ("Holocaust celebrations," as the memorials were ironically called by members of the drama club.)

I was a member of the "club to immortalize," and I also played a Polish cook in the performance of the history of the uprising. But in fact, a partition still remained between me and the others, a zone of silence so dense that, to this day, I don't know which of the children of the Krakow community members were children of Holocaust survivors and which were children of parents who emigrated to Palestine before the war. If there were any children of survivors, no bond was formed between us. We didn't talk about it. We remained isolated, caged in the sealed biographies of our parents.

There were other bridges too, almost subterranean ones, which, as far as I recall, were not formulated explicitly. The bond with the literature teacher, the poet, Itamar Yaoz-Kest, who survived as a child with his mother in Bergen-Belsen. In high school, there was only his influence on

* Code name for Gusta Dawidson Draenger, resistance fighter and author of diaries written while imprisoned by the Gestapo in Krakow.

my literary development and a sense of closeness, a sort of secret look between "others." Only later did I read his poems of "the double root" about his split childhood "there" and in Israel, and his story describing, as he put it, a little girl who looked like me, the daughter of survivors. And there was the love affair with the boy in my class, whose delicate smile on his drooping lower lip looked like the "different" smile of the literature teacher. His father, the lawyer, submitted reparations claims to Germany in those days—close enough to the seductive-dangerous realm. My complicated relations with that boy paralleled the shock of discovery of Kafka; and along with the tempest of feelings of fifteen-year-olds, that forbidden, denied, inflamed relation had a pungent mixture of eros and sadism, a tenderness and an attraction to death, and above all, metaphysical dimensions that pierced the abyss of dark feelings which somehow was also part of "there."

In my childhood, when Mother was an omnipotent entity within the house, I couldn't "understand" her. Later, when she became the authority to rebel against, the enzyme necessary to cut the fruit off from the branch erected a dam of alienation and enmity between us; I couldn't identify with her, with her humanity. There had to be a real separation. I had to live by myself. To go through the trials alone. To listen slowly to what was concealed.

(An amazing example of the layers of memory and for-getting was revealed to me as I wrote *The Name*. The only detail I borrowed in the novel from things I had heard from Mother was a story of the heroism of a woman who succeeded in escaping from Auschwitz-Birkenau, and when she was caught and taken to the Appelplatz, the roll call area, she managed to commit suicide. I also borrowed the admir-ing tone in which Mother spoke of the event—only later did I discover how it had served her as a model. I created a bio-graphical-fictional character, a virtuoso pianist, and invented a name for her, Mala, which I turned into Amalia, the name of the heroine. Years later, as I was finishing the book, I came across a written description of the event in Birkenau and discovered that the name of the woman was the same as the name I had "invented," Mala—Mala Zimetbaum.)

Then came the move to Europe, to Paris. To study for the doctorate and to write literature intensively. I went to the Paris of culture, of Rilke, of Proust, of Edith Piaf. But in 1972, soon after I arrived, the film *The Sorrow and the Pity**
by Marcel Ophuls was released. When the screening ended in the cinema on the Champs-Elysées, I emerged into a dif-ferent Paris, into a place where that mythical war had gone on. I understood that here, on Rue de Rivoli, beneath my garret room, German tanks had passed (ever since then

* (1970) Documentary film exploring average French citizens' memories of Nazi occupation.

they began to inhabit my dreams); I understood that the description of the French as a nation of bold underground fighters and rescuers of Jews—a notion I had grown up with in the years of the military pact between Israel and De Gaulle's France—was very far from reality. The clear, comforting borders between good and bad were shattered for me, and so were the simple moral judgments mobilized for ideologies. Here, far from a post-Six-Day-War-Israel, secure in her power, far from the official versions of Holocaust and heroism, a different time was in the streets, a time not completely cut off from the war years. Here, for the first time I experienced the sense of "the other." As a Jew, as an Israeli. Wary of revealing my identity at the university that served as a center of Fatah* activities, trembling in the Metro once as I read the Israeli newspaper, *Ma'ariv*, when someone called it to my attention: "Mademoiselle, somebody spat on your jacket."

Distance also allowed a different discourse with my parents, especially with Mother. In the weekly letters, without the daily tension of life at home, a new bond was formed, between people who were close, who were beginning to speak more openly with one another. Even my clothes in the European winter, in the "retro" style, began to look like the clothes in Mother's old pictures from Poland, like her hairdo

---

* Arabic term for the Palestinian Liberation Organization, founded in 1964.

in the photo next to the jeep from Hanover, when she served after the war as a commander in Aliyah B,* the Brikha,† camouflaged in a United Nations Relief and Rehabilitation Administration uniform. Poland, Hanover, suddenly turned into places that were much closer, more present than the little state on the shores of the Mediterranean.

On the first Holocaust Memorial Day in Paris, I decided to stay in my apartment all day and to cut myself off from the street that lived by its own dates, for example, Armistice Day of World War I, the "Great War" that took place at the same time of year. I spent the day reading works on the sources of Nazism, on the roots of anti-Semitism, on the German nationalism of Wagner, rehearsals of whose *Parsifal* I had attended at the Paris Opera.

That summer, on a tour of Europe, an accident forced me to stay unexpectedly in Munich for three weeks. And then the blank spot that filled the heart of the European map for me—Germany—the blank, untouchable spot that sucked up all the evil, also fell. Here, next to the beer hall of "the Nazi buds," where some Israelis had taken me, in what was obviously a sick gesture, there was also an opera, where Mozart was performed, and there were wonderful museums, and parks.

* Code name given to the illegal immigration of Jews to Palestine in violation of British restriction (1934–48), distinguished from Aliyah A, the limited Jewish immigration permitted by British authorities in the same period.
† (Hebrew) Organized attempt to collect Holocaust survivors in Europe and bring them to pre-state Israel, resulting in three hundred thousand survivors reaching Israel (1944–48).

The forced stay in Germany and the Yom Kippur War the following autumn, which I spent in Paris facing the brightly lit Champs-Elysées while my dear ones were in mortal danger, proved to me that there is no refuge in the soothing distinctions between "then" and "now," between "there" and "here." And I also understood that there is no racial difference, imprinted at birth between "them" and "us," nor can we Jews hide behind the fences of the Chosen People. And that, in every person, the murderer and the victim potentially exist, blended into one another, constantly demanding separation, every single day, with full awareness. I understood that I could no longer hide behind the collective, ready-made definitions of memory. That there would be no choice but to embark on the journey that is obstinate, lonely, and full of contradictions.

Germany, France, Europe: What is in that culture, in its roots, mixed with the gold of the baroque and the flickering brasses of symphonies; what is in the squares, in the churches, in the ideologies that allowed what happened? Prepared it? Didn't prevent it? What inflamed the hatred? What repressed it under pious words of morality? What fostered it in the heart of religious belief? What prepared it in the tales of God that man told himself to justify the outbursts of his evil instincts under the disguise of *imitatio dei*?*

* A religious concept by which man finds virtue resembling God.

And what still exists right before my eyes? Keeps on happening?

How to draw the borders between good and bad with a thin scalpel under a microscope? How to distinguish anew, here and now? All the time?

And what is the terrorizing persuasive force of tales and of their metamorphoses into theologies, ideologies? How to struggle with forgetting, with denial, without whitewashing, but also without reiterating the same stories, without inflaming the same evil instincts? How to tell responsibly?

Jarring questions that filled me, that nourished my research, my theatrical productions, my literary writing, but did not yet touch Mother's hidden place.

I spent the summer of 75 between Princeton and New York, collecting material for my doctorate, reading the works of Rebbe Nahman of Bratzlav in the old Jewish Theological Seminary library, and in the evenings, swallowing the plethora of fringe theater, jazz, and transvestite clubs in the international bohemian life of Manhattan. And thus I met that young violinist who had fled Poland, and was working as a cabdriver. A handsome young man from Krakow. Krakow? A place where people live?! The summer romance was a way to confront the profound seduction of the past stamped in me, as well as the depths of my femininity.

One day that summer, my aunt, Mother's sister-in-law, came to my apartment in midtown Manhattan. I knew her vaguely from a visit she had made to Israel years before: After the death of Aunt Tonka in Tel Aviv, this aunt from Queens, the widow of Mother's second brother who perished in the camps, was her last living close relative. She had survived Auschwitz and her young son was hidden with a Christian woman. After the war, my aunt and her son emigrated to New York.

That day, on the balcony on the thirtieth floor, facing the roofs of midtown Manhattan, my aunt spoke in broken English only about "then" and "there," a here and now didn't exist, as if we had never left there. She and the Polish pop music at night melted the last wall of resistance. Now I had no excuse not to translate my preoccupation with the subject into action, no excuse not to go to Poland.

In late October, after the administrative alibi was concocted in Paris, I left. Ready. And not ready at all.

I was not ready for what I would find or for what I wouldn't find. I was not ready for the fear. The fear of returning to the strange hotel room at night, the primal fear that I would starve to death, which impelled me to eat nonstop, completely violating the rules of kashrut which I had observed ever since I came to Paris to study, eating nonkosher with the dispensation "allowed during an emergency," that I granted myself (insolently?). Not ready for the fear that rushed me in a panic straight from the visit to Auschwitz-Birkenau to meetings with Polish artists and bohemian parties. I was especially not ready for the complexity of my responses, for their force. For what was revealed to me in "the living laboratory" I had poured by myself. The contradictory burst of fascination and revulsion, alienation and belonging, shame and vengeance, of helplessness, of complete denial . . .

When I returned, the letter to my parents was a first attempt to look at what was revealed, to talk. The restrained language of the letter reflects the difficulty of going beyond the taboo, hoping they would understand through the silence. That different, new discourse with my parents accompanied us throughout the years until their death. A discourse of closeness, of belonging, of acceptance beyond the generational differences.

The sense of belonging—along with my parents—to the "other, Jewish story" revealed in the depths of the journey only intensified in the following years, as the doors to the centers of European culture opened to me, as I devoted myself to writing. But at the same time, the understanding that it is impossible to go on telling as if nothing had happened also grew. Understanding that, after Auschwitz, there are no more stories that do not betray, there are no more innocent stories.

And what about Mother's shrouded "story"? Details continued to join together in fragments. For years, here and there, she mentioned events, some in conversations with me, some in conversations with others, which I chanced upon. I listened when she spoke, and she spoke little. Never did I "interview" her; never did I ask. I respected her way of speaking, as well as her way of being silent. Even after I returned from Auschwitz, I didn't think she had to report or that I had to, or could, "know." I learned from her the lesson of telling in silence.

I heard the first fragment of a chronological description from my mother under extraordinary circumstances. In the autumn of 1977, she was summoned to give testimony in a German court in Hanover. I accompanied my parents to the trial, sitting with my father in the gallery and seeing Mother, with her special erect posture, surrounded by the black robes of the attorneys. In her fluent German, she described the Plaszow camp, where Jews from the Krakow ghetto were taken; she pointed authoritatively at the maps. Her voice trembled only a moment when she came to the description of the Kinderheim, the children's home in Plaszow, where children were taken from their parents. In a few words, she dealt with the *aktzia*,* told how all the inmates of the camp were taken out to the square while an orchestra played lullabies, to see how the SS loaded the children onto the trucks that took them to the gas chambers. She was asked what was the name of her son, and how

* (German) Common nickname for the deportation and murder of Jews.

old he was at the time of the *aktzia*. She replied with an effort, "Marek. Eight years old." The prosecutor asked for a momentary recess, and then the questions resumed. (That prosecutor accompanied us when we left, apologizing in shame for the accused, the deputy of Amon Göth,* the commander of Plaszow, who was absent from the courtroom "for medical reasons . . . ")

A few years later, Mother tried to dramatize the story of the revolt of the women in Krakow at the vocational high school where she taught, wanting to bring the subject close to her women students. She worked with Father on the script and developed original ideas of staging designed to increase audience participation. But, during the rehearsals, she developed such a serious skin disease, clearly as a reaction, that the doctor advised her to stop the production.

The presence of the Holocaust receded completely in her last months, as she struggled with the fatal cancer that was discovered in her. Death was too close to think about the old dread—at any rate, that was my feeling as I stood at her side admiring her yearning for life, the audacity, the amazing black humor, which restored the dimensions of human absurdity even in the most difficult situation. The day before she lost consciousness, she spoke a lot, in a stupor, in Polish. What did she say? Was she still living

* (1908–46) Austrian war criminal found guilty of murdering tens of thousands of people. He was executed by hanging.

there? I couldn't go with her. I remained alone, by her bed-side. Then, as I was massaging her feet, those feet that had marched in the death march through frozen Europe, I was struck with the simple knowledge that it was to Mother's struggle, there, that I owed my birth.

I heard Mother's "story" only after her death—death that always turns a loved one into a "story" with a beginning and an end. During the shiva, Rivka Horowitz came to Jerusalem from Bnei-Brak. A woman with bold blue eyes, whom I knew only by name. Rivka Horowitz was one of nine women, all of them graduates of Beit Yakov, the ultra-orthodox school for girls in Krakow, whom my mother joined in the ghetto, despite differences of education and ideology. The ten women, the *zenerschaft*,* supported one another in the ghetto, during the years in the Plaszow camp, in Auschwitz-Birkenau, throughout the death march, and in the final weeks in Bergen-Belsen. For three years, they hadn't abandoned one another; together they fought exhaustion and disease, lived through the selections, until all of them survived. "There was strength in them. Moral strength," Mother explained when she and Father, both of them members of the liberal, secular Mapai party,† assidu-ously attended the celebrations of the friends in Bnei-Brak.

* (German) A unit of ten, used ironically.
† (Hebrew) A left-wing political party, the dominant force in Israeli politics until it merged with the Israeli Labor Party in 1968.

At the shiva, I heard from Rivka for the first time about that period. She spoke for a few hours—out of responsibility to tell me—and left. And after that, we didn't meet again. Later on, when I was almost finished writing *The Name* (and after Mother's death, it seemed to me that, more than ever, the novel spoke of a "there" that was lost forever), came the first information about the family property in Krakow. Apartment houses, a button factory . . . Property? There? "In the regions of delusion?" And then, the name that had been common at home, Schindler, which suddenly became a book and then a film, and turned into a general legacy the story of the rescue of Mother's cousin and his wife, and Mother's refusal to join the list of workers in the enamel factory in order to stay with Marek.

Then, one evening, the telephone rings in Jerusalem, and on the other end of the line, in English with a thick Polish accent, another member of that *zenerschaft* introduces herself, Pearl Benisch, who published a book in 1991, *To Vanquish the Dragon*, with the full story of the group (from the author's religious perspective). A copy arrived on a Friday. On the Sabbath eve, I sat with my two little daughters in the living room and picked up the book. I leafed through it distractedly, until I came to the deportation of the children of the Kinderheim. And then I fled to the other room so my daughters wouldn't see me, and there I burst into sobs I didn't know were hidden inside me. A weeping that arose from there. Mine? Hers?

Until dawn on the Sabbath, I read for the first time the story of Mother, in chronological order, dated, revealing the few facts I knew situated in their context. Even the description of the *goggle-moggle* with sugar that she had secretly made for Marek in the sewing workshop, where the women from Plaszow worked, smuggling the treat to the child when she came back to the camp. And how one day the Jewish supervisor discovered her stealing the egg for the drink, and threatened to turn her in. And how she stood before him in mortal danger, and accused him in front of all the workers of the sewing shop of being a traitor to his people. I read how, in the *aktzia*, the liquidation of the children's home, against the horrifying background of lullabies, Mother burst into the square toward the SS men who were pushing the weeping children onto the trucks. She shouted to them to take her with the child. And how her friends, the women of the *zenerschaft*, held her with all their might, pulled her back. I read about the sisterhood between the women in the group, about the pride, the unbelievable humor, how with astonishing freedom they maintained their humanity in the camps of Auschwitz-Birkenau. They and many other women and men were described in their humanity, facing yet finding ways to elude the crematoria. How they succeeded in putting on makeup to get through the selections, how they sneaked the weak women out of the line of the condemned, how they secretly lit candles at Hanukkah and held a Passover Seder, and how, after the death march from Auschwitz to Bergen-Belsen, they still managed to laugh together when they got the wrong-size prison uniforms. I read, frozen stiff, how, in Bergen-Belsen, Mother dared to be insolent to the female SS officer with the pride she still had left, surviving the public whipping, which few survived, without shouting "so as not to give the SS the pleasure." Between the pages, the figure of Mother returned to me, cheering the women in Auschwitz with stories of her visit to the Land of Israel, singing them songs of the homeland on their muddy beds, where they fell exhausted with typhus and teeming with lice in Bergen-Belsen. Suddenly I understood one of the few stories Mother had told me about the camps, how she would sing to herself Tchernihovsky's poem: "You may laugh, laugh at the dream, I the dreamer am telling you, I believe in Man, and in his spirit, his powerful spirit," emphasizing with her off-key voice the words: "I believe in Man, and in his spirit, his powerful spirit . . . "

Mother's "story." Discovering it in the heart of the journey to what was stamped inside me. Discovering it now in the middle of life, when I myself am a mother, and older than she, the young woman and mother who was there.

"Mother's story," or maybe only milestones around what will remain hidden.

PART II: LETTER FROM
THE REGIONS OF DELUSION

Paris, November 2, 1975

My dears,

Back home—what a relief!

A week in Poland is like a year, like years, like a moment. Ever since the visa was approved, a week before the trip, I felt as if I were facing an operation. I was waiting for something to stop me, for an iron curtain to block the way. And even in the dark, when the bus took us from the plane to the airport in Warsaw I still didn't believe that the distance between me and Poland would be swallowed up just like that, in a few steps.

Your letter, which reached me just before the trip, was a lifeline in moments when the dizziness intensified; in moments when there was only a definite absence of my imaginary picture of those places, when instead, there were only the long lines in gray raincoats; in moments of awful loneliness, when there was no one to shout at; in moments when I didn't believe I could finally get on the train and leave that madness behind.

How to tell, and wasn't there any chronology? How to live that over again?

Wroclaw. A dreary city and a theater festival. I was ejected into the darkness in the heart of an empty field. That's how it began. Night in the hotel. An enormous radio, and voices from Russian, Polish, Czech, and Hungarian stations. Stifling heat from the furnace, the chambermaid, a blond Gentile woman, fills the bathtub for me. In the soap box and in the closet are roaches. A strife-torn night in dreams and a grayish morning. The outside was stopped by the curtains. Crowds of people with rubbed-out faces. A few old cars. Awful cold. Fog.

How to leave the room and go into that reality? How to be a "tourist" in it?

Wroclaw. In the display windows, rows of laundry soap in coarse packages. Cooperative restaurants smelling of cabbage and sweat. In the festival offices, full ashtrays, organizers with sleepless faces. And then a writers' café, in Kosciuszko Square, and it was as if I had come to a kind of Jerusalem before I was born, from the thirties, a Jerusalem I lived from books. With that blend of provincialism and culture. Waitresses dressed in black with starched aprons, newspapers in wooden frames, cigarette smoke, grave discussions about art, literature, politics, metaphysics. The soft tones of a language that is so familiar, so close. The intonations, the gestures, the excited seriousness.

An international festival—a few days of devotion to joy, before the regime returns to its everyday gray.

And I, a stranger at the celebration. Only an "alibi" for another mission, which no one in fact has assigned to me. Yes, a few addresses for it's impossible-not-to-accept-with-a-letter-to-take before setting out. Backs of houses, yards covered with trash and rubble. Staircase supported by boards. Number 72, apartment 9A. Two old people in the doorway. A kitchen black with soot. Examining me, the letter, with a scared look.

Sneaking back to the ongoing celebration, just so they won't find out.

It's only because of sloppiness that they haven't yet arrested me.

And then, early one misty morning, wrapped in a coat, at the railroad station. Among hundreds of people in a line. Buying a ticket to Krakow with black-market zlotys . . . to the regions of my real trip.

Getting off the train, and simply walking into the light-flooded square among ancient buildings, whose carved facades are sparkling in the sun. Walking among the other people on the boulevard with the autumn chestnut trees, on Planty, Mother's route to the tennis courts. Autumn leaves struggle on my shoes. Entering the Rynek Square resounding around itself. The Renaissance arches, the Sukiennice market in the middle like an island in the heart of a lagoon of light, the breeze rising from the Virgin Mary Church . . . all those names, with a soft "r" as I ("wonderful child!": the only two words I understood in the foreign language) would accompany Mother to the nightly suppers on an aunt's balcony with a smell of down comforters and the saltiness of the sea air on hot Tel Aviv nights, when friends from "there" would gather. All those names, when the conversation would climb in the foreign tremolo, and in the café downstairs, the yard of the building, the cards would be shuffled on tables. The places frozen in slides on the wall of the high school, in commemorations held with a sudden frenzy. Places that were stopped in the thirties, with an amazed look of some Jew who came on the camera by mistake . . . The warm-cool air caresses the fur of my coat, my face, moves the parasols over the flower vendors' booths.

The road rises to a high hill overlooking the city and the Vistula River. Above, the Wawel Castle covered in ivy burning with autumn leaves. And here, on the slope, along the banks of the Vistula, the way to Paulinska Street, Mother's street.

The three o'clock twilight lingers and softens. Mothers with babies in buggies at the river (Mothers and babies? Still? Here?). Paulinska Street. On the secret side of the street the wall of a convent, and behind it fruit trees. Some-one passes by on the corner. A woman in a heavy coat and old boots. Number eight. The staircase floored with blue tiles. A list of tenants in fountain pen. First floor on the left—a strange name. The door is locked. On the first floor a balcony. Closed glass doors, covered with lace curtains.

To throw a stone at them mischievously, a schoolbag on the back and stockings stretched up to the knee? As I used to walk over there, dressed carefully by Mother, among the children giggling at my different clothes. To sit down at a steaming lunch, close to the breath of forefathers I never saw? Only crumbs of medicines and old lipsticks in drawers of the aunt who died. That silence. The quiet of houses. Take a picture. A picture of air? Quiet. Across the street, in the convent garden, a bell rings. Children pour out of the gates of the school, climb on the fences, chew on apples.

Spotted facades and the street spins. Not far from there, Kazimierz, the Jewish quarter. The soot of trams on the doorsills of the houses. In the windows of the reform syna-gogue, the "Temple," spiderwebs, and in the yard a tangle of weeds. In the alley of one of the houses is a blurred sign in Yiddish, "Prayer house." The big synagogue is empty and whitewashed. Turned into a museum. Only a guard passes by like a shadow along the walls, and two fragments of tiles from back then are embedded in the entrance.

It's late now. I wander along the track to the cemetery. Here at least I am sent by permission, to an address that does exist, to the graves of the family. The gate is closed. There is no one to ask. Everything is closed.

An evening full of mist. Suddenly the trams are hurrying. The voices of the flower vendors in the Rynek are swallowed up in the fog. To go to the reserved hotel? In Krakow? Like going to a hotel in Tel Aviv instead of returning home. The desk clerk scurries up to help: "Yes, of course, Madam, here's the bus schedule to Auschwitz. From the town of Oswiecim, you have to go on foot a bit."

On the table at the entrance of the hotel are old newspapers. Two elderly lady tourists are interested in a jazz festival that may not take place. And there, at the foot of the stairs, on the way to the room, the movement that had swept me up ever since early morning stops. No, just not to return alone to the gigantic radio in the strange room! I buttoned the coat and went out in pursuit of a dubious rumor that I'd heard. Slawskowska Street. Maybe . . .

And indeed, in the dark, in Yiddish, among the artisans' signs, a small address: "Mordechai Gebirtig* Culture Club." A door at the edge of a yard. A doorman sits at the entrance. And in the depths, in the gloom, a few frozen figures are playing cards, gazing vacantly behind the wooden frames of newspapers. "Israel!" the doorman sits up straight, leads me with sudden importance to the "board" room. Five

---

* (1877–1942) An influential Yiddish poet and songwriter, best known internationally for his song "*S'brent*" (It is Burning). He was killed by a Nazi bullet in the Krakow ghetto on Bloody Thursday (June 4, 1942).

wrinkled faces rise up to me: "Israel!" They sit me down in the middle, following my efforts in a mixture of basic German, a few words in Yiddish, and gestures. They nod at length in deep wonder at every word, assault one another in noisy arguments. Finally, they answer together, in a strange chorus: "Ha! Yes, Poser's daughter! Poser and Abeles," they nod: "Buttons, buttons!" "Yes, buttons," I affirm; "a button factory." "The Hebrew high school," I continue. "Yes, the high school. Now a Polish technical school." The Christian cook serves me a sandwich with a lot of bread and a cup of tea. They dismiss her with the superiority of a bygone age, and urge me: "Eat, eat." For a moment, they go back to their business. The "chairman" is dictating a petition to the "secretary" about the cultural situation. To whom? On behalf of whom? Still? Like those stenciled pages in cellars and photographs of pale-faced choirs that were presented every Holocaust Memorial Day in the glass cabinets of the school. I attempt to explain; they will certainly understand that it's impossible to get on a bus and simply ask the driver in a foreign language to tell me where to get off for Auschwitz. They certainly have their own ways of getting there. And indeed, it turns out that tomorrow, a "delegation of rabbis from America" is about to come, and they will go in a special bus. When will they arrive? When will they go? Where are they now? Impossible to know. Got to wait.

I want to sneak away from them now, back to the big square. To go into an anonymous café with drunkards. To be swallowed up there. But they hang onto me, wrapped up in their coats, accompany me to the hotel. Argue with outbursts of rancor, finally declare that the "secretary" will come to "guide me" tomorrow morning. They all press around, shake my hand. Downtrodden faces. So small. In threadbare coats.

In the room the suitcase is waiting, with a few things. Makeup, passport. Will have to go on and move it. Impossible to hide in the suffocation under the blanket.

The next morning, before I have time to ponder the other world in my dreams, the "secretary" is already here, dragging me with soft-limbed domination. Turning me around in dark streets, getting on and off trams, talking incessantly in the incomprehensible language, as if to herself. And I plod behind her, bending down to her, making an effort.

In Kazimierz, on the bench across from the synagogue, the doorman of the "Mordechai Gebirtig Culture Club" and two old men are already waiting for me. It's not clear if they're beggars or rabbis. They came to welcome the "American delegation." The doorman waving as he approaches, "Yes, yes!" One of the old men hurries me, opens the gates of the ancient synagogue of Rabbi Moshe Isserlish. For a minute, a separate hush. The figures that follow in my wake remain beyond the fence. A small building whose heavy walls are leaning, and a white courtyard. Inside the synagogue, there is still a warmth among the wooden benches, around the Ark of the Covenant. On the tables are old prayer books. Black letters. And in the small enclosure crows land on the ancient tombstones sunk in the mist. For a moment the past seems to continue with all its softness, without any obstacle, in that distant murmur, up to the morning covered with mist, to me.

And the doorman is already rushing me hysterically; he arranged with the gatekeeper of the Miodowa cemetery to be there, to open the gate. Hurry, hurry, got to get back in time for the "delegation of rabbis!" And thus, in single file, the doorman limping, the muscular Christian gatekeeper on his heels, and I behind them, we march between long rows of sunken, shattered gravestones, covered with mold. Names, names. I recite to them the names I've managed to dredge up from my memory, "Poser, Mendel, Groner." Tombstones in long rows whose edges vanish in mist and piles of fallen leaves. Many strange names. Don't find. A Christian woman with legs swathed in bandages rinses the graves with boiling water, raises her head wrapped in a turban to us: "Yes, Groner, saw it once . . . maybe there." I still hold on, persist in reading the names, seeking under piles of leaves. But the limping doorman and the gatekeeper behind him are already hurrying out. We didn't find. No maps. No books. No witnesses. Mission impossible. Only a delusion of mission. And time is limited.

Meanwhile on the bench the number of idlers and "rabbis" waiting for the "American delegation" has grown.

According to the doorman, they are already in Krakow and will arrive very soon. Maybe you can find out in the hotel when they'll arrive? No, impossible to know. I break away from the doorman, tell him I'll come back in a little while, he should beg the rabbis of the delegation to wait, and I hurry to Wawel Castle, for the visit that was arranged. On the streets people in gray coats, buses, trams. You can even eat an apple. The body goes on functioning over the abyss between the worlds. And when I come back from the royal palace, from the halls with waxed floors whose walls are covered with embroidered tapestries of feast and forest, devoured by torments of treason, I run down the slope carpeted with fallen leaves, back to Kazimierz, to my Jews. From the end of the street, the doorman stumbles toward me. He drops his hands in a gesture of dismissal; "Well, the American delegation . . . a call came that they didn't leave America. Well, the fog, they didn't leave America."

Empty. No one there. Even the idlers who were waiting on the bench have gone home.

Entrusted with the last mission, the doorman rushes me into the community organization offices. Second floor, a smell of boiled potatoes, a few old people with tin plates and spoons. Even the bright light filtering from the shutters doesn't bring the scene in the room any closer. Around the enormous table sit the activists of the "congregation," their chins leaning on their hands, and their crutches leaning on the chairs. A few old portraits on the walls. At the head of the table, Mr. Jacobovitch, an irascible Jew, head of the community organization. The mutual curiosity dies out after a few sentences, and after I am given the travel arrangements I slip out impolitely. I also flee from the kosher meal of mashed potatoes on a tin plate and the ritual washing of the hands in a stained sink, to Sukiennice Square, to the light, to the fancy café with red velvet chairs and torte powdered like the cheeks of the Polish women. Here you can shout aloud that maybe everything is a delusion, that maybe there were never Jews here.

And it was as if a shout burst out of me in the evening at the performance of *The Night of November Ninth* by Stanislaw Wyspianski,* directed by Konrad Swinarski. Mythic characters singing against a background of a burning horizon. The tricolored flag of the revolution waves over the stage, and the audience is galvanized. A moment of naked yearning for freedom is revealed, of metaphysical emotion, a moment of a personal world despite the constant oppression. Something so familiar, so close in temperament, in gestures. Such belonging. Belonging?

An old car. The shaved nape of the driver's neck stuck in a cap. Poplar trees, autumn fields. I am in the back seat, huddled in my coat. On the way to Auschwitz.

And perhaps you should be silent about that trip. Not talk about the yellow flowers, the gravel in the sun, the

* (1869–1907) A Polish playwright, painter, and poet who linked modernism with the Polish folk tradition.

chatter of Polish cleaning women who laughingly point out to me that my trousers are unstitched. My trousers? On what side of the barricade?

How to write you about the strained pacing in an attempt to grasp something about the remnants of constructions—from archaeological digs of thirty, not two thousand years ago. To understand the chasm separating sanity and madness with barbed-wire fences. The house beyond the fence, half a mile away, was always there, with the same smoke in the chimney and the same geranium pots behind the curtains. And here?

How to write about the dark steps with a group of Polish high school students on them. The wall of liquidations between two blocs. A barred window. A few fallen leaves scattered on the sill. Expressionless walls in the gas chambers, the iron doors of the ovens. Polish sky. Between the chambers, in the corridors, photographs and numbers. Printed columns of names. And the silence of another morning now. As when I held my breath, a girl of six or seven, in the schoolyard for a whole minute, through the whole siren, so that I'd be dizzy when I intoned the words, six million.

How to write you about the forced march through the tremendous extent of Birkenau Camp. About the dampness still standing in the abandoned blocs, between those three-tiered wooden bunks, and the straw sacks on the dirt floor. How to imagine Mother with that silent madness. Mother.

A shaved head in nights of hallucinations, nights among packed bodies. How to put Mother into one of the gigantic photos placed along the railroad track. How to force myself to imagine her in this emptiness?

Polish earth. Small autumn flowers. The driver waits. Dozes in the sun in the car.

And maybe all the questions are not right. For it's impossible to understand. Not even at the end of the journey to this stage set. Impossible to understand without the fear of death that catches the breath, without the palpable threat on the flesh. Impossible to grasp death from all the hundreds of photos. Maybe only the heaps of empty shoes are still hovering between life and death. There I finally recited the kaddish.* Kaddish over heaps of shoes.

And maybe all the questions start only after the shoes also crumble. Beyond the crazy stage set of death, which will always remain incomprehensible. And maybe all the questions begin, only with the silent emptinesses of now. How to go on living in a world that had turned into the enemy. With the fear stamped in the blood. With the constant paranoia. "*Arbeit macht frei*."† How to live within the world and outside it. In the flow of its life and in the flow of other life and eternity. How to go on nevertheless believing in man, how to take the beloved head in the arms.

* (Aramaic) The prayer recited at funerals and by mourners.
† (German) "Work brings freedom," the sign over the gates of Auschwitz.

In the afternoon light, trivial thoughts pass through the head. Impossible to pretend suffering; that would be hypocrisy. Impossible to go back to the past—clinging or accusing—that would be the triumph of the past. There is no escape from the constant questions to be asked now, impossible to flee from them to the images frozen in the photos.

And in Warsaw, in the ghetto, there aren't even any ruins where the imagination can take hold for a moment. There are no stones left from times past. Only concrete blocks built a few feet above the ground, above the ruins and the mounds of corpses that weren't even cleared away. To hold your head in your hands and shout. Life goes on. Cars in parking lots, a few poplar trees on the sidewalks. And that emptiness. Only the lip service of a memorial with the pathos of socialist realism, and a Jewish museum behind the building of the Communist party. The director of the museum and his secretary, two Jews with bowed heads, show me a building excavation out the window. "Here was the great synagogue of Warsaw." And the cleaning woman smiles like an accomplice in a crime, and points at the exit to the guest book full of emotional comments. Gray cement boulevards and gigantic statues of soldiers with forged chins. Impossible to believe that there was once a different life here. Only in the nationalized Desa stores* are there scores of Jewish objects. Hanukkah lamps, synagogue

* USSR chain of stores.

menorahs, spice boxes. Objects with price tags. No, there is nowhere to return. The whole thing is only a delusion. Deceptions of the imagination. In my head crushed fragments of all the artistic creations resound, the assemblies, the recitations that tried to convey the other reality to me, and they only increase the distance.

The rain doesn't let up. An awful cold penetrates the clothes, makes you shiver. Warsaw—a gray horizon by day, and gray in the pale neon lights at night. The trip back seems like an illusion, like opening the camp gate and being outside. The unbearable loneliness, the unrelenting suffocation.

Only the friendship of my acquaintances, Polish theater people, supports me in the hours before the departure. Figures between reality and dream. Alicia in her theatrical clothes, waving her hands like a Chekhov character. And Andrzej with ironical humor, in fragments of literary French, with the credo from Communism to the surrealism of Witkiewicz. Fervent confessions in small apartments when tomorrow is unknown, and only the dream is left. Like the awakening appreciation for Bruno Schulz, thirty years after he perished, like worshipping the theater, the word spoken from the stage, received with a sigh. Like the clandestine grasping of Catholicism.

Childhood memories extend between Mediterranean summers and alleys in northern cities, woven in the dreams of Polish romantic literary heroes, shrouded in the sounds of the language and open accounts of the blood of the dead.

Life in a pre-time is always present, in the double look at all the places. Always through the other place I belong to, where you don't come on journeys. A wiped-out place, condemned to delusion, where I will never be able to put to rest the wandering of existences.

With relief I finally board the train. Sleeping cars that came from Moscow with a conductor in an undershirt and a stifling smell of sweat and orange peels. A twenty-four-hour trip to Paris, like a day of fasting. To another world? At midnight, the train passes the East Berlin station. Signs in Gothic script "Welcome to the Democratic Capital." On the platform is a white line three feet from the cars. Soldiers in riding boots with German shepherds and submachine guns are standing at regular intervals. A patrol of two soldiers goes through the train. Another patrol checks between the wheels with flashlights, and another one marches on the roofs of the cars. Maybe someone has succeeded in escaping. A white line, soldiers, and a train. Only the site of madness or freedom has changed.

Back in Paris: The clear sky, department-store advertising instead of propaganda slogans. Quiet. The silence of the room. And that drawn orbit of where you two are so close at hand. "Flesh of my flesh."

Beloved father and mother, I press you to my heart, and once again am gathered in your arms.

LA PROMENADE, TRIPTYCH

PART I

"For the time being we can rest here," said Monyek Heller when they reached the bench at the edge of the beach. "It's nice here, opposite the ocean." And the soft sound of the Polish words in his mouth was accompanied by an interrogative lilt.

"Fine, fine." Lusia Taft nodded, the same little smile on the face of her short body expressing part submission, part uncertainty, and part effort to convey thanks.

"We can wait here for the others to arrive," said Monyek, hastily pulling a large handkerchief from the pocket of his light-colored suit and sweeping it over the bench before indicating to Lusia, with a ceremonious flourish, that she should sit down.

He smoothed his pants and sat, straightened his slender back, crossed his legs, and placed his hands one on top of the other on his right knee. Then he raised his chin and sur-

41

veyed the broad beach, which was covered with mist and bedecked with a string of little flags at the water's edge, dancing in the breeze in the distance.

Lusia carefully straightened the skirt of the suit she had had specially made for the voyage and sat down on the light green bench. A woman has to try to look her best, and she set her bulky purse down neatly, next to the knees peeping out of her skirt.

"A beautiful day," said Monyek, and he went on looking at the ocean lying motionless at the bottom of the slope, as if it had been put to sleep by the mist that had shrouded the oceanside resort all day long.

"Yes, a beautiful day," confirmed Lusia.

And they sat for a moment without talking, gazing in front of them at the ocean. The white sand came all the way up to the bench, penetrating the little holes in the weave of Monyek's leather loafers and sticking to the heels of Lusia's broad shoes. Monyek straightened his hands neatly on top of his right knee and Lusia held her full body a little more erect than necessary.

"Really, everything is beautiful here," she suddenly announced shifting in her place. "I don't know how to thank . . . "

"No need, really, no need." Monyek Heller drummed with the fingers of his right hand, and the signet ring on his finger glittered.

"The beach is so big," continued Lusia, a shade dramatically, turning her head from the glitter of the ring to the glint of the water at the edge of the beach. "After so many years a person forgets."

"Yes, yes," replied Monyek, and after a while he added, "I'm a regular here every weekend from April to June, twelve years already. It's good for my lungs. In the summer I go for the cure to Montecatini, and last winter I tried the baths at the Dead Sea. It was good. No question about it." He shook his head slightly from side to side and then added, "And we met there too. That was also good."

They both smiled, as was only fitting at such a moment. Monyek patted Lusia's right hand lightly with his left hand, after which he replaced it on his knee.

"Very nice what they've built there. Every convenience." Monyek recommenced.

"Yes, yes, very grand," replied Lusia in an animated tone, taking care to keep her purse upright.

"No question about it, they've done great things there in Israel!" summed up Monyek.

"No question about it," replied Lusia.

And neither of them had anything to add, especially since the country in question appeared no more real at that moment than the tiny figures of the bathers moving like dots at the edge of the water.

"I didn't ask yet how things are at the shop," said Monyek, and his fingers resumed their drumming.

"June isn't the best time of the year for wool," replied Lusia, "But as long as the shop stays open I'm not complaining."

"That's right," agreed Monyek.

"A person needs a break every now and then. After a while you get tired—you know how that is. It isn't easy with all that tension all the time," said Lusia, and her heavy voice hovered in the air for a moment around the light green bench at the edge of the shore.

Behind them rose the cliffs with the grand summer houses, preserving a nostalgic fin-de-siècle royalty in their ornate façades. And on the beach the white planks of the walkway led right down to the changing booths at the edge of the ocean.

"No, it isn't easy . . . " repeated Lusia after a moment.

"It isn't easy," said Monyek too, and after a while he asked, "It's not too hot for you . . . " He almost said "Mrs. Taft," but thought the better of it and concluded on a more familiar note, "Lusia?"

"No, it's very pleasant here," replied Lusia, and she went on to ask the question that was expected of her. "And how are things at the workshop?"

"Could be worse. We did quite well this season." said Monyek. "We're busy with the new autumn models already. Plenty of worries, as usual, but for the time being, not bad at all."

He raised the hand adorned with the signet ring, tugged

at the knot in his fine woolen tie, and straightened his crossed knee. Then he replaced his hand, and finally he let his knee fall back into its former position.

"And why shouldn't it go well?" he went on. "The children are fixed up. And ever since Rouzia died I try to do whatever the doctors say."

And after a short pause, during which he made a number of little pecking motions with his sharp chin, he said, "And now we can begin again together, no?"

And the drumming of the fingers of his right hand on his left kept on moving the signet ring up and down.

"Yes. There's quite a lot in common," said Lusia.

"*Nu*,* like we already agreed, wool and ladies' wear go together quite well," said Monyek with a laugh, uncrossing and recrossing his thin legs.

Lusia laughed too, and then there was another silence which was not even oppressive, so peaceful was the expanse of sand receding into the water. For a moment Lusia lifted her orthopedic shoes out of the sand, and then she placed them back again.

"Good afternoon to Mr. Heller and Mrs.——"

"Taft!" cried out Monyek, making haste to rise to his feet and turning to face the roly-poly person approaching them along the esplanade at a pattering run. His full face,

* (Yiddish) Multipurpose interjection, often analogous to "well?" or "so?"

almost completely hidden behind his sunglasses, beamed all the way up to the crown of his bald head, and his whole appearance proclaimed he was on vacation: from the perforated white shoes hopping back and forth to the open mesh of the shirt flapping around his thighs and the white hairs peeping out from the broadness of his sunburnt chest.

"Sitting on the beach, eh?" he called as he approached. "Just the two of you!" And a burst of heavy laughter rocked his body.

"The lady is from Israel. From Tel Aviv," said Monyek when the laughter of the holiday-maker had somewhat subsided.

And Lusia turned herself around with the erectness appropriate to the occasion and held out her hand: "Pleased to meet you."

"Hirshel Feingold!" Monyek hurriedly announced.

The latter skipped from his place and lowered himself rapidly over his round belly to Lusia's hand. "The pleasure is mine entirely, mine entirely," he said, and he went on, smacking his lips admiringly, "So, she's from Israel? Very nice, very nice!"

"This is Hirshel Feingold, who I already told you about," said Monyek, as if for Lusia's ears but loudly enough to let him know that his name had already been mentioned between them.

"Oh ho! What did you tell her already?" cried Hirshel in mock alarm, and although he made a sign with his hand as if there were no need for them to tell, it was evident from his smile that he was waiting eagerly to hear.

"*Nu*," Monyek shrugged his shoulders in mock resignation. "I told Mrs. Taft a little about your business interests on the international scale, your branches in Hamburg, New York, London, South Africa—*nu*, the whole list, more or less. Also how right after the war, while we were still in the DP camp, you already began making money in real estate and steel."

"Let's not talk about it!" mumbled Hirshel Feingold, already shifting himself to the other side of the bench. And before Monyek had time to finish saying politely "Sit down with us, Hirshel," Hirshel was already sitting and wiping the sweat from his brow with a pudgy hand. And leaning forward stiffly over his paunch he went on in the same breath, "They didn't open La Promenade yet? It's already after five! Everybody should be here in a minute. Henrietta's arriving in a minute too. I left first. I couldn't stand it any more shut up in those four walls. When we come here I always say: 'You have to get the most out of the ocean air, and not stay shut up in your room!'"

And after breathing in a noseful of the air, he turned to Lusia Taft and said, "So, the lady has come to us for a little rest?"

Lusia was embarrassed, and Monyek began to mutter, "No, the lady . . ."

But Hirshel Feingold went on talking without waiting

for a reply, "Nice, nice, very nice. And I'm just leaving next week for my hotel in Natanya! You know the Hotel Repose there? Not bad, eh? I put it up in 62. *Nu*, I've got some in Eilat and Nahariya too. We have to support the state, no? Not a bad living. But plenty of problems, as usual in Israel. *Nu*, so how can you do business with Jews already?" And he burst into laughter, which wobbled his shoulders, convulsed his belly and legs, and in the end set his hands shaking too, at first opposite each other and then clapping against each other. Monyek too hurried, if a little late, to join in the laughter and Lusia nodded her head after them.

"Henrietta! So you came out at last!"

Hirshel reared his head and waved his chubby hand at a tall woman in a narrow-skirted suit, who was limping toward them along the esplanade. Even from a distance it was evident that it was an effort for her to put one foot in front of the next, and it was clear that in spite of Hirshel's explanations they had set out from the hotel together.

"Come on, come on, meet some new people!" Hirshel went on calling out toward her, without rising from his seat.

Lusia watched with pursed lips as the woman approached, and then she stood up and held out her hand. "Lusia Taft. Maiden name Mandelstein."

"Pleased to meet you. Henrietta Feingold," replied the woman, and her handshake fell away.

Monyek rose and bowed. "Hello, Mrs. Feingold."

And the haggard woman limped around the bench, passing close to her husband's back in order to sit down in the empty place beside him. But before she got there Hirshel mentioned, "I saw Arlette riding on the beach!"

And turning quickly back to Lusia and Monyek as if he were addressing an audience, he said, "Our daughter's fantastic! She knows how to live!"

"Arlette's riding?!" cried Henrietta, and sat up in alarm.

Hirshel dismissed her cry with a downward flap of his hand and was about to turn back to his audience when the sound of opening parasols was heard, and immediately afterward iron chairs being banged down on a terrace: At last La Promenade café had opened its doors for the afternoon service which, more than anything else in this oceanside town, was taken as supreme proof of the fineness of the weather.

Hirshel Feingold leaped to his feet and said, "Over to La Promenade, everyone!"

And he hopped off to make sure to get their regular corner on the terrace. Right behind him, Henrietta lifted her body from the bench and stumbled after with anxious concentration.

Lusia Taft and Monyek Heller remained sitting where they were a moment longer, but Hirshel Feingold was already urging them on from the café terrace: "Monyek, Mrs. Taft. What's the matter? What are you waiting for?"

He himself was busy dragging the round iron tables together and waving chairs about in his short arms.

"Coming! Coming!" called Monyek Heller in reply, and he went on sitting on the bench with Lusia Taft, facing the white sand and the little fleet of sailing boats whose solid bellies were cut out like blue silhouettes in the mist. In the end he bent over Lusia and offered her his arm.

In the meantime Hirshel Feingold had completed his corner arrangements. The chairs stood untidily around the tables, as if at the end of a party. In the corner, next to the canvas partition that marked the boundary of the café premises, Henrietta sat erect, preoccupied, and silent. And as if to fill the vacuum left by her silence, Hirshel sent cries of encouragement toward Monyek and Lusia, who were coming up from the beach with heavy steps, and waved both hands at two couples who were approaching along the esplanade. "Over here! Over here!"

Among the other people strolling up and down the esplanade, bordered on one side by the café façades and on the other side by the expanse of sand stretching into the mist and the ocean, there could be no mistaking the destination of the two couples who were making for the corner of the weekend regulars at the La Promenade café: The deliberate tread, the way in which the ladies gripped their purses as if they were travelling bags, the embarrassment with which the man at the right buried his hand in the pocket of his loose-fitting suit, or the determined air of well-being surrounding the checkered cap set jauntily upon the head of the man at the left. The latter approached arm in arm with his yellow-haired wife, the bright pink of whose outfit matched her husband's vacation air. Next to them, the couple at the right appeared somewhat ill at ease.

"I see we have new visitors today!" Hirshel Feingold declared happily.

And the owner of the checkered cap hastily dropped his wife's arm and pushed the new couple forward as he announced: "Mr. and Mrs. Harari from Ramat-Gan."

"Mrs. Taft from Tel Aviv." Hirshel promptly took his turn as sponsor.

And in the hubbub of greetings and handshakes filling the café terrace with Polish sounds, Monyek bent over to explain to Lusia, indicating the man in the checkered cap and the woman in the pink suit, "The Honigers, from Paris. In synthetic underwear. A first-class business."

Hirshel Feingold made impatient gestures with his hands. "Sit down, sit down!" he cried. "Why are you standing?" And he pointed at the circle of chairs placed chaotically around the tables.

Mr. Honiger gallantly pushed the chair closest to him toward Mrs. Harari, whose gray hair was gathered into a bun behind her head. Mr. Harari drew in his legs and folded himself into the chair next to his wife. Mrs. Honiger sat down beside him like a genial pink chaperone. Last to be seated were Monyek Heller and Lusia Taft, and Lusia turned her chair carefully around so that she could see the shore from where she sat. Only Henrietta did not get up while all this was going on; she remained in her place next to the canvas partition in the corner. Mr. Honiger jumped quickly to his feet again and held out his hand to Henrietta over the tables. And Hirshel Feingold called out to the assembled company, "*Nu*, what's everybody drinking?" He beckoned the waiter with a proprietary air.

The waiter, who was apparently well acquainted with the weekend regulars, folded his hands across the white napkin over his arm and waited while Hirshel counted off the orders one by one:

"Tea, coffee, lemonade," and in the end he turned to Henrietta, who said, "I'll have tea with lemon," as if she were committing herself to a fateful decision.

Hirshel sent the waiter off, and all agog at the new audience he turned toward them and made a number of unclear, agitated motions with his hands. In the end he burst into a long laugh of contentment. When he'd finally calmed down, and all the others too had finished signaling their participation in the mirth, Hirshel wiped the moisture from his forehead and said, "*Nu*, not bad here in Europe, eh?"

Marek Harari nodded his dark, pointed head and lowered it with a smile. "For sure."

"Good, good," continued Hirshel, without paying any attention. "Good, all this reminds me of the joke . . . "

But Gusta Harari, who felt the need to add something to her husband's words, leaned over to Henrietta and said full-throatedly, while Hirshel was still telling his joke, "We only came because of the Honigers. They insisted we come here on the way back to take a rest at their ocean resort."

And when Henrietta made no response, Gusta continued, turning to Lusia and smiling at her confidingly, "Otherwise how could we possibly have afforded it?"

Hirshel burst out laughing, and his laughter was echoed automatically by Mr. Honiger and Monyek Heller. Marek too stretched his face in a grin, but his eyes remained sunken. And Henrietta, who had almost disappeared behind her husband's gleefully agitated limbs, dismissed the joke with a pursing of her lips and shifted slightly in her chair.

The waiter arrived with a nickel-plated tray loaded with jugs of tea and coffee and tall glasses of lemonade. He put the order down according to their instructions in front of the people seated around the table. Hirshel placed his thick hand on the tab and closed his fist around it.

"It's on me!" he cried.

Mr. Honiger and Monyek Heller attempted to protest. Hirshel Feingold waved both his hands in the air and proclaimed again and again, "No arguments! It's on me!"

They all smiled in enjoyment and stirred their drinks. The mist on the beach thickened and brightened, almost hiding the glitter of the ocean from the eyes of the people sitting on the café terrace. A number of vacationers strolling along the esplanade turned their heads curiously at the sound of the hubbub.

Mr. Harari lowered the china cup from his mouth to the saucer and said, "The espresso is really very good here."

"The lemonade, too." Mrs. Harari followed suit.

Hirshel gave the little cup of coffee engulfed between his hands an energetic stir and said, with the self-satisfied air of a man who has just brought a business deal to a successful conclusion, "Yes, yes, not bad. Not bad at all."

And Henrietta, bending her whole height over the table, squeezed the lemon in her tea with tiny movements, making innumerable clinking noises with her spoon against the side of the china cup.

Mr. Honiger took advantage of the pause in Hirshel's stream of words and began, "A government auditing committee came to my factory in Paris—five Jews, can you imagine?"

"I'd rather not . . . " began Monyek Heller, wrinkling his forehead slightly, but Hirshel replaced his little cup on its saucer with a bang, slapped both hands down on the table, and burst tempestuously into the conversation. "Ten days ago when I flew . . . "

"And what was your maiden name, may I ask, Mrs. Taft?" Mrs. Honiger turned with a yellow-haired smile to Lusia Taft.

"Mandelstein," replied Lusia, and she leaned over the table to make herself heard, "Lusia Mandelstein."

"Mandelstein?" repeated Mrs. Honiger, thrusting her pink-clad bosom toward her. "And where are you from, Mrs. Taft?"

"Tarnów," replied Lusia. "And you, Mrs. Honiger?"

"Chrzanów," answered Mrs. Honiger.

"My late husband had family from there," said Lusia.

"What was the name?" asked Mrs. Honiger.

"Romek Taft," replied Lusia.

And Mrs. Honiger nodded her head. "We were in Israel until 55, and then we moved to Paris."

"Yes, yes," Lusia, too, nodded understandingly.

Hirshel's laughter drew to an end like a roll of thunder receding into the distance, and rubbing his fat hands in satisfaction he turned his attention to the newcomers.

"So what brings Mr. and Mrs. Harari to us at La Promenade?"

He flung this out of the corner of his mouth at Henrietta, who was still squeezing the lemon against the side of her china cup. "They're from Ramat-Gan. Having a little vacation in Europe, eh?" He answered himself, and he was already turning to Monyek Heller about to begin a new subject when Mrs. Honiger said suddenly, "Tell them! Tell them!"—and her pink earrings swayed excitedly on the lobes of her ears.

Hirshel turned to face her with an air of pleasurable anticipation, and cried, "What, not for a vacation? So you came to get rich at our casino, eh? We have to beware of our Israelis—one of these days they'll break the bank!" He waved a fat finger at them.

"It's not important, Hella," said Mr. Harari to Mrs. Honiger. "Really it's not important."

"What's the matter? It's nothing to be ashamed of! You can tell them," Staszek Honiger joined in from the other side of the table. "We're in a free country here!" And he tried to laugh in order to make his encouragement more emphatic.

Marek Harari lowered the long head sticking out of his suit, and the skin of his neck tightened. He shrugged his shoulders and said in a reflective tone, "What difference does it make? We were in Munich." And again he concluded with a weary shrug of his shoulders. "Now we're on our way home."

"Really, there's nothing to be ashamed of!" cried Hirshel gleefully. "The mark's a strong currency, and in business you do whatever's necessary. It's nothing to be ashamed of!" And his last words were swallowed up in loud laughter, which tossed both his hands about and ended up in a rapid, triumphant glissando.

Monyek laughed loyally with him, and Lusia smiled too. But Mr. Honiger persisted all the same in his explanation. "No, they . . . "

"We gave testimony in Munich," said Marek Harari, and

he concluded with a limp, downward flap of his hand, "You know what it's like."

"We arrived on Monday," continued Gusta Harari, "and finished on Thursday. On the way back the Honigers offered us a rest in their flat by the ocean."

"On Thursday it was all over, and we went to Paris," said Mr. Harari again.

"Who was the case against?" Monyek Heller asked quickly, in an apologetic tone.

"Heineke," said Marek Harari, and he shook his pointed head.

"Heineke?" asked Lusia Taft.

"What?" asked Monyek.

"No, I thought . . . " said Lusia.

"He wasn't there!" exclaimed Gusta Harari bitterly.

"Who wasn't there?" asked Monyek Heller uncomprehendingly.

The Honigers, who were already acquainted with the facts, shook their heads in an aggrieved way. Gusta Harari clutched her purse, although it was already firmly ensconced in her lap and said as if she were reciting, "When we arrived they told us that he was sick and couldn't stand up to the strain of the trial. We waited in the hotel for two days without going out. They told us to be ready to testify the moment he recovered. On Thursday they said they didn't know when he would recover. They took us to court, and they wrote our testimony down in the protocol. They said that in the meantime they were collecting background information. Then they let us go, and it was over. Fela and Abel Gutt were with us too. From Holon. You know them maybe? Also from Bochnia. They went back on Thursday. We're going back tomorrow. It's over," concluded Gusta Harari, and after a moment she suddenly burst out with a fury ill-suited to the pleasantness of her gray bun, "What good did it do anyone? Tell me—what?"

"Don't say that, Gusta," scolded Marek Harari, as if continuing an old argument.

"Yes, I know," Gusta took a firmer grip on her purse, and her face woke momentarily from its darkness. "It's important, but who to?"

"What are you saying, Gusta?" asked Mr. Honiger in a soothing but perfunctory tone, "What are you saying?"

"The Germans? They dragged us all the way there to tell us he was sick," continued Gusta Harari obstinately. "Our children, perhaps? Better they shouldn't know. And anyway, they don't care. They're too busy with other things."

Marek Harari nodded his head, as if he knew all about it and was resigned to the situation.

"Yes, yes," said Lusia Taft to herself.

"Gusta, really, you shouldn't upset yourself." Mrs. Honiger threw all the weight of her genial presence into the calming effort. "It's enough!"

And Hirshel Feingold drummed his short fingers restlessly on the tabletop and burst out laughing. "They wrote about my painting collection in the papers! You know what they said? The condition for a good investment in art is ignorance!"

"We've never spoken about it to Arlette!" Henrietta Feingold's voice cut through her husband's laughter. "Never!" She jabbed her head forward for a moment and then relapsed into her stiff-backed silence.

"Yes." Mr. Honiger quickly confirmed, without knowing exactly what, as long as it put an end to the discomfiture. "Yes, today it's something else again; you can't go on forever living . . . with . . . " And since he didn't know how to go on, he fell silent.

Monyek Heller said, crossing his legs more firmly, "We deserve a little peace and quiet too, don't we?" And he smiled carefully at Lusia. But she didn't notice his declaration because at that moment she was absorbed in the movements of the tiny figures on the edge of the beach.

Mr. Harari put his lemonade glass down next to the flask of water standing on the table. His glass was dry, and the water flask was empty. He shifted slightly in his chair and drew in his neck again, as if he were trying to fold himself up inside his loose suit.

Mr. Honiger straightened his checkered cap and directed a polite and perfunctory "Hmm" toward Hirshel Feingold.

In the end Monyek Heller said, "I think we'll go eat now. What do you say, Mrs. Taft?"

Lusia looked back from the beach and replied, "Yes, yes."

"Excuse us," said Monyek, and when he stood up he too saw the figures gleaming in the dense light of the sun hanging low in the yellowish mist.

Lusia carefully straightened the skirt of her suit and patted her hair into place with a heavy hand. She bent down and shook the hands of the people sitting around the table, and when she parted from the Hararis she said, "If we don't see each other again, have a nice trip."

Hirshel, who stood up in order to supervise their departure, made haste to intervene. "You'll see each other, you'll see each other," and he concluded with a patronizing laugh: "We don't say goodbye so quickly over here."

Monyek stretched over Henrietta's hand. "Mrs. Feingold." And he escorted Lusia off of the café terrace.

No sooner had they taken a few steps than they heard Hirshel turning to the people left sitting around the tables: "What's the matter? Why shouldn't Monyek marry Mrs. Taft from Tel Aviv? Maybe he should better start running after young girls at his age?"

"Not so loud, Mr. Feingold." Mr. Honiger tried to silence him.

"What's the matter? What's the matter? It's nothing to be ashamed of," Hirshel went on obstinately thundering.

Lusia Taft turned her head away from the esplanade for

a moment and saw the Hararis sitting between Mr. and Mrs. Honiger on the terrace of La Promenade, shrinking a little between the checkered cap and the cheery pink suit.

They walked up the esplanade, climbing steeply above the bluff. Lusia Taft tugged at her jacket which tended to crease at the back. With one folded arm she clasped her purse to her body and with the other she beat time heavily as they walked, as full of concentration as if they'd just set out on a long strenuous march. Monyek Heller walked beside her with long steps. His head nodded to itself, and his fingers rubbed incessantly together as if he were rolling something between them.

"What time is it?" asked Lusia.

"After seven," replied Monyek.

"I've lost sense of time." Lusia lifted her head. "I'm not used to such long evenings any more."

"Yes, yes," said Monyek, and he contemplated the ocean which had grown somewhat darker and bluer. His fingers went on rubbing each other, and the signet ring shone as it moved back and forth. He nodded his head and seemed about to say something to Lusia. But he merely smiled distractedly and she smiled mechanically back. Her swollen feet, supported by the buckles of her orthopedic shoes, alternately clattered and dragged on the esplanade.

At the top of the bluff they passed a stone balcony

jutting out from the heights of the esplanade like a pier suspended in midair. A black iron mast pointed at the shifting clouds above it. They passed it without stopping.

"That's the Map of the World Observatory," said Monyek, and he laughed a little, as if to apologize for the fact that they'd walked all the way up the hill without exchanging a word.

"Yes," replied Lusia, as they started down the hill toward the row of restaurants.

The ocean air was dense and briny, and the foreign voices spread over the esplanade. She tightened her grip on her purse and looked at the people sitting on the restaurant terraces, at the festive little flags, and at the slender women walking in front of them along the esplanade on their high, pointed heels. Then she looked at Monyek Heller walking by her side, his head lowered toward the pavement.

"We'll eat out tonight, eh?" said Monyek in the end. "We're on leave from the hotel, we only took half-board." And he creased his lips in an effort to laugh.

"*Nu*, gefilte fish they won't give us, but we'll try to make do with French cuisine." He went on, stressing the words "make do" and tightening his tie in order to affirm his membership in the world of the oceanside resort.

But the restaurants were full, and the tables outside on the terraces were all occupied too. The diners sat crowded together nibbling at shellfish piled in pale heaps, and it was evident from the satisfaction with which the waiters turned Monyek and Lusia away that business was prospering this weekend at the beginning of summer.

"Here!" Monyek pointed at an empty restaurant where the tables were all set for dinner, and signaled Lusia to go in in front of him. The waiter who hurried out to meet them shrugged his shoulders and said without enthusiasm, "We're waiting for an organized group, but if you like we can set one more table for you outside." He pointed to a table for two standing at the edge of the terrace, close to the glass wall of the restaurant.

"That's quite satisfactory," said Monyek, and cleared the way for Lusia between the tables. He brought up the rear and helped her pull up an iron chair and slide it beneath her, as she straightened the skirt of her suit. Then he pulled up the chair on the other side of the table and sat down.

Lusia sat up straight in order to proclaim it was a very nice place. She hesitated for a moment and decided in the end against hanging her purse on the back of the chair. She placed it on her knees and clasped it to her bosom.

"Do you think we'll see the Hararis again?" she asked.

"Why?" asked Monyek.

"I want to give them a letter for Israel. For my children, you know," said Lusia.

"Don't think about it." Monyek dismissed the subject with a smile and picked up the menu that was standing on the table, and presented it ceremoniously to Lusia. "I'll

translate for you," he announced, emphasizing the importance of the occasion.

"Yes, yes." Lusia opened the folded cardboard menu.
"Because if something happens they won't know where to
get in touch," she said, and stared without seeing at the list
of names in the unfamiliar language.

"Don't worry, really. We're here now. There's a beautiful view, and also . . . " But Monyek didn't finish the
sentence.

"Yes, very beautiful!" Lusia quickly agreed, turning
down the corner of the menu.

Monyek took his eyeglasses out of his jacket pocket and
put them on. The thin lines of the gold frame gave him a
scholarly air, arousing speculation as to what he might have
become if he hadn't gone into ladies' wear. For a moment he
concentrated on trying to find the exact Polish equivalent
for the names of the dishes on the menu, while Lusia bent
stiffly forward, all attention. In the end she said, "Really, it's
all so expensive. The meal, the trip . . . "

Monyek interrupted her with a complacent air. "*Nu*,
please. There's no need . . . " And he beckoned to the
waiter.

Lusia closed the menu and replaced it carefully on its
stand, just as it had been before.

The waiter wrote down Monyek's order, removed the two
menus, and rapidly poured water into their glasses. Monyek
smiled contentedly at the efficient service and glanced at

Lusia like a wealthy man showing off his possessions. Lusia took a slice of bread and pinched off a piece between her fingers. She filled her mouth and chewed slowly.

Monyek smiled and said, "*Nu*, it's not easy to find the right woman."

"What?" Lusia stopped chewing.

Monyek rested his hands on the table, but quickly drew back when the waiter arrived and deposited their orders.

"Bon appétit!" he said to Lusia Taft, as if they were in the habit of exchanging such civilities. He poured a little wine into his glass, tasted it, and then poured for Lusia.

"Good, the wine is good." He smacked his lips like a connoisseur.

Lusia stuck her fork into the steak and began cutting into it slowly.

"We can still begin again!" said Monyek.

"Yes," replied Lusia. She put the meat into her mouth, praising it as she did so. "The meat is very good."

"Yes, it's good," said Monyek, stretching his legs under the table, and he turned to the plate in front of him.

They sat chewing, on either side of the table, sipped their wine, and resumed their chewing.

"Nothing like this in Israel, eh?" said Monyek, scraping the meat from the bone. He straightened his woolen tie and continued, "Everything is so tense there. A hard life. Here at least a person can live in peace. Afford to take a break at an oceanside resort from time to time."

The waiter stopped a number of vacationers who were about to sit down on the terrace of the restaurant.

"Inside if you wish. Outside all the tables are booked!" he said, as they tried to argue with him, pointing in an aggrieved way at Monyek Heller and Lusia Taft.

When their dessert was placed before them the sun had already set, and the bluish light of the long evening had enveloped the terrace. The esplanade was full of weekend vacationers, and their light clothes were also covered with blue dust.

They had already placed their spoons next to their glass dishes and Lusia had opened her purse and removed her lipstick in order to freshen the red smear on her lips when a large tourist bus drew up in the street in front of the restaurant. It maneuvered clumsily until in the end it parked right outside the terrace, completely hiding the fishing harbor on the other side of the esplanade and the play of light and evening on the clouds.

The waiter hurried to the entrance of the terrace in order to welcome the people descending from the bus two by two and talking loudly to each other in German. At their head marched a short, plump man who seemed to be the tour organizer. The waiter ran behind the customers and showed them to their places. The organizer made jokes, and from time to time he slapped the shoulders of the people sitting down. And in the space of a few minutes the terrace was packed full of couples sitting in crowded rows. And all alone in the corner, as in a tiny enclave, stood the table of Monyek and Lusia.

The manager of the restaurant came out. He was wearing a black suit and a bow tie in honor of the occasion. He too received a friendly slap on the back from the organizer, and then he hurried off behind the waiter to collect the orders from the diners and to see that everything was to their satisfaction. The waiter deposited bottles of beer and wine along the tables, which was greeted with cheers and an outbreak of loud chattering.

Monyek screwed up his napkin and wiped his mouth with it several times. The waiter banged their glasses of tea down in front of them and hurried off with his tray to serve the German diners.

"*Commun za va?*" The man sitting closest to their table at the end of the row of diners turned his face toward them with a broad smile.

His words directed the attention of the people next to him to the couple sitting on the terrace, and they all turned smiling faces toward Monyek and Lusia.

"*Non parler français.*" A second man, wearing a brown-checked suit, joined in the conversation, laughing with the full weight of his body.

The wives of the two speakers stared at Lusia with the respect due to a native of the place. One of them, whose hair stuck out like a fair ball around her head, pointed to her lips in order to indicate that she didn't speak the language, accompanying this gesture with a low laugh.

The first man, who apparently knew a greater number of words, went on. "*Nous bataillons ici, comprenez? Bataillons? Krieg.*"* He pointed to the people sitting around the tables and broadening his smile and shaking his head from side to side in an exaggerated way as if telling a story to children, he continued, "*Maintenant ici. Visite. Visite. Avec Frau. Comprenez?*"† he asked, and burst into friendly laughter.

And as if waiting for a signal to join in, the man in the three-piece brown suit and the two women also laughed, nodding their heads at Monyck and Lusia.

The waiter returned and unloaded his tray.

When Monyek picked up the bill lying on the table, the Germans were already tackling their first course. Monyek placed some bank notes on the saucer with the bill and rapidly counted out the coins for the waiter's tip. He stood up, Lusia stood up too and gathered her bulky purse to her bosom.

The man with the square chin turned toward them, smiling through his chewing and said, "Au revoir Madame, au revoir Monsieur!" He waved his hand at them.

The two women also turned their heads, and the man

---

* (Distorted French and German) "We soldiers here, understand? Soldiers? War."
† (Distorted French and German) "Now here. Visit. Visit. With wife. Understand?"

in the brown suit quickly wiped the grease off his lips with his napkin before calling out in a broken accent, "*Au rouvour! Au rouvour!*"

Monyek and Lusia squeezed their way to the exit along the space left between the outer wall of the restaurant and the chairs of the diners. Monyek exited first and Lusia, treading heavily in his wake, had difficulty finding a place to plant her orthopedic shoes. Sounds of pleasure and chewing filled the terrace. Laughter accompanied the raising of beer and wine glasses and the jokes and funny anecdotes. The people seated next to the wall of the restaurant turned their heads to look after them enjoying their food and the delightfulness of the occasion.

They walked along the esplanade, and the German voices from the restaurant terrace were gradually swallowed up in the noises of the evening. The restaurants were still full and the empty shells of white shellfish stood in piles. A troop of youngsters in black leather jackets and tight boots passed them. Monyek and Lusia made their way through the people standing next to the brightly lit shop windows, and when they approached the Municipal Casino they saw women in evening dresses and fluffy fur capes stepping out of black limousines and disappearing up the marble staircase like huge moths, leaving a train of darkness behind them.

As they reclimbed the bluff opposite the Map of the World Observatory, Lusia glanced at Monyek and saw he was looking down at the pavement. They walked without saying a word. Lusia's heels clattered in the intervals between his steps and she clutched her bulky purse to her bosom still, as if she were leaning on it for support as she walked.

The evening spread toward the street lamps, and down below, on the beach next to the water, the twilight trembled. Lusia shifted her purse from hand to hand and drew the lapels of her jacket together to arrest a sudden chilly breeze.

"Did the doctor send you to have tests?" she asked.

"Yes," grunted Monyek.

"What were the results?" continued Lusia.

"He said there was nothing to worry about for the moment. But still, I should start taking things a bit easy. Get used to the idea that things aren't what they used to be."

"But he was optimistic, no?" persisted Lusia.

"Yes I think so," answered Monyek, as they passed the balcony of the dark observatory.

After a second, Lusia said, "That's encouraging."

The lamp on the post rising from the observatory was unlit, and the balcony with its shell-shaped stone balustrade hung over the ocean like the shadow of obsolete grandeur.

"I don't know what kind of world we're living in!" Monyek suddenly burst out, and his sharp chin trembled. "How they can come here without being ashamed, I don't understand!"

"Don't think about it," said Lusia almost to herself.

"There are some things I just don't understand," continued Monyek, striking his head passionately with the palm of his hand. "I just don't understand!"

"Romek also used to say that people should learn from the past. He was a man with values," said Lusia. "But how long can you go on thinking about the same thing?"

"The cheek of it!" continued Monyek, and his voice grew tired.

"Really Monyek, you shouldn't upset yourself," said Lusia, and there was a certain tenderness in the way she beat time with her free hand.

"Yes," said Monyek, and he tugged distractedly at the hem of his jacket.

They descended the esplanade from the top of the bluff and the observatory, and Monyek's steps resumed a subdued tapping between Lusia's heavy strides.

"Yes, there are still a few good years in front of us," he said.

"Yes," said Lusia, and nodded her head.

When they turned their backs on the light that was still clinging to the ocean, Lusia continued, "Whatever happens, I'm getting some repairs done in my apartment. The marble on the sink top in the kitchen, and the balcony blinds."

"Whatever happens," Monyek repeated after her.

They walked along the spacious street of the oceanside resort. The ornamental trees planted between the street lamps on the avenue swayed in the evening breeze.

"Remind me to take a sleeping pill when we get to the hotel," said Monyek.

"All right," said Lusia.

When they were approaching the hotel, in the light of the elegant display windows, Monyek Heller turned his head and stole a quick glance at the woman who was walking beside him with a heavy tread.

The next morning, Monyek knocked on Lusia's door, as agreed.

"Mrs. Taft. Lusia." He leaned into the door in the hallway.

"Yes yes," answered Lusia, who was already awake in her bed.

"Sorry but I have to hurry you up," continued Monyek behind the door, "Hirshel Feingold called and invited us to a celebration. I don't understand exactly of what."

"I'll be ready in a minute," replied Lusia, and she sat up in bed among the big pillows and sheets, which were still starched, although she'd already slept in them for two nights. The big room was dim, and underneath the high ceiling unknown smells were circulating. The night had left a murky residue in her. She propped herself up on both elbows and descended slowly from the high bed. She pulled the curtains apart and pushed the balcony shutters open. On the sunlit wallpaper countless shepherds and shepherdesses with their flocks rested under pale blue trees. They climbed to the ceiling and disappeared behind the big wardrobe.

She went into the bathroom and rummaged in her old cosmetic bag in order to take out the toilet articles that for some reason she hesitated to leave displayed in the place intended for them, on the glass shelf glittering underneath the mirror. She turned her back—for years now she'd avoided looking at herself undressed in the mirror—and mechanically finished fastening her corset and pulling on her orthopedic stockings. Then she turned around, and with a few vehement strokes she painted vivid color over the slit of her lips. When she'd finished powdering her forehead and cheeks, she threw her things back into the cosmetic bag and straightened up her crushed coiffure.

When she'd finished dressing, she sat down for a moment on the corner of the high bed, ready to leave with her bulky purse already in position on her knees. For a moment she puzzled about the Sabbath here, which stretched on into Sunday, and then she immediately bent stiffly over her purse, with her short legs dangling, and made sure that she'd not forgotten to put in her compact. And while her hand was kneading the guts of her bag, she also made sure she had her pills. She stood up, wondering apprehensively whether she'd creased her skirt, and straightened the bed-spread, whose motif of sailing ships reconfirmed the vacation atmosphere. From the window she saw the two trees in the hotel garden. She crossed her hands under her bosom around the strap of her purse and left the room.

When they'd finished eating breakfast Lusia took the lipstick out of her purse again and roughly repaired the drawing around her lips. Monyek crumpled the napkin and placed in on the table. He rose from his chair and approached Lusia to offer her his arm. A heavy smell of perfume rose from her body. He was wearing his brown silk tie today, and it shone with the richness of earth between the lapels of his jacket.

When they stepped outside he was troubled by the pressure in his chest, which had grown worse since the chestnut trees had come into blossom. This morning too the sky was covered with mist and the air was not yet really warm. Only a few bathers had ventured onto the white beach, and the little flags strung between the lifeguard stands waved limply. They hastened down the wooden walkway on the beach in the direction of the café La Promenade. Monyek leaned over to tuck his hand in Lusia's arm alongside the strap of her purse. Lusia patted her hair, and every time she put her heels down on the wooden planks the noise of her dragging feet eased for a moment the uncertainty of her deliberate tread.

At the other end of the wooden walk Hirshel Feingold, who'd come out to meet them, was already waving his hands at them, like a brightly-colored, capering stain on the open beach. He covered the distance between them at a scampering run and the coconut trees emblazoned on today's shirt swayed violently from side to side.

"They wrote about it in the newspaper!" he shouted, spreading a big page in front of them.

When he reached them he grabbed Monyek by the arm, pumping it up and down in agitation. "I took the Hararis to the casino last night to let them have a look. But with Hirshel there's no such thing as just watching. I started playing with a hundred and ended up breaking the bank! They shut the casino down when I won!" He burst into expansive laughter, and hit the rustling paper with the back of his hand. "Take a look!"

Lusia and Monyek bent over the newspaper and saw a dark picture of Hirshel embracing two uniformed croupiers against the background of the roulette table, his round face beaming.

Still laughing, Hirshel snatched the paper away, disappearing for a moment behind the sheet spread between his two hands and emerging again with a gleeful face after he folded it. Once again he grabbed Monyek's arm and started pulling him along.

"First we'll have champagne at La Promenade," he announced, "And after that lunch at the Excelsior.

Hirshel never misses a chance for a celebration!" And he was off again, running in front of them with his low shoulders swaying from side to side, the coconut trees on his shirt swaying right along.

On the terrace of La Promenade Henrietta stood tensely, twisting and untwisting the strap of her purse. Next to her stood a man in a striped suit and a brown hat. Monyek presented him to Mrs. Taft. "Please allow me to introduce—Mrs. Taft, Mr. Zucker."

"Pleased to meet you," said Lusia with her polite smile, and she shook hands with Henrietta, placing one foot in front of the other in order to indicate that as far as she was concerned the walk was over.

"He was with us in the same DP camp," whispered Monyek into Lusia's ear. "Also in ladies' wear. He never comes before Saturday night—can't afford to shut his business down earlier."

Lusia nodded her head understandingly and went on smiling at the owner of the brown hat.

"Arlette hasn't arrived yet!" Henrietta burst out.

"But Mrs. Feingold," said Mr. Zucker soothingly, obviously for the umpteenth time, "You know what youngsters are like today. Really, there's nothing to worry about."

But Henrietta was not appeased and she went on wringing the strap of her purse with small, rapid movements.

From the table Hirshel clapped his hands. "Mrs. Taft, Mr. Zucker, Monyek! We're all waiting for you!" and he signaled to the waiter who hurried to uncork the bottles of champagne standing on the table.

They sat down in their usual places, except that this morning Mr. Zucker trying to be useful seated himself between Lusia and Henrietta. Hirshel rose to his feet and poured the frothing liquid into the glasses with a flourish.

Marek Harari choked a little and coughed. Gusta Harari hurried to pat him on the back. Marek's sallow face flushed like an elongated copper platter. When his coughing had subsided he raised his face apologetically and smiled at Hirshel Feingold, who was already refilling the glasses. Hella Honiger laughed, and her broad bosom looked more authoritative than ever inside its pink jacket. Mr. Honiger nonchalantly emptied his second glass of champagne, and Lusia whispered in confidence to Monyek, "I'm not used to drinking so much."

"A little celebration never did anybody any harm," replied Monyek, clinking his glass ceremoniously against hers.

"Us too! Us too!" Staszek Honiger called out from the other side of the table, stretching across to clink his brimming glass against Mrs. Taft's and half rising to his feet as he said, "We wish you the . . . " But he sat down again without finishing his sentence. They haven't said anything official yet, so maybe it's better not to be too much in a hurry, he muttered to himself, and in order to cover up his over-hasty gesture he addressed the rest of his toast to Henrietta:

"We wish only happiness to our young ones!" And he gulped down the rest of his champagne, holding his jaunty checkered cap in place with the back of his hand.

Hella Honiger chimed in quickly, "Yes, the young ones should be happy!"

Mrs. Harari too raised her glass in a burst of emotion and announced, "The young ones shouldn't suffer; they should live in peace! That's the most important thing. In peace and quiet!"

"Drink up! Drink up! Don't be lazy!" urged Hirshel Feingold, lifting another bottle from the tray, which was already covered with a puddle of champagne, and impatiently filling the glasses. "You should've seen the people in the casino last night; they were fit to burst!" he said, pouring the champagne onto the table without paying any attention to what he was doing. He added, shaking with laughter, "I think they won't let me into the casino again! Ha ha!"

Marek Harari leaned toward Mrs. Honiger and said something to her. Gusta Harari nodded quickly in agreement. Mr. Honiger agreed too, and hastened to say, "We have to start moving already. The Hararis have to be at the railway station."

"Yes, yes," said Marek Harari, jumping up from his place. Gusta rose immediately after him and stood beside him, ready to go.

Hella Honiger said, summing up with an official air, "It was a pleasure!"

Lusia Taft made haste to rise after them. "I'll give you my son's telephone number. If you could get in touch . . . "

"Out of the question! You're not going like that!" Hirshel cried, clapping his hands for the waiter. "We're all going to see our Israelis off. *Nu, nu!*" He urged Mr. Zucker on, signaling him to support Henrietta, fumbled with his wallet, and rapidly placed the bills in the waiter's hand.

Lusia Taft finished writing the telephone number down on a piece of paper and bumped into her chair as she hurried around the table to Gusta Harari. The waiter folded the bills into the pocket of his vest, highly satisfied with the generous tip he'd received to judge by the number of times he bobbed his head at the celebrants as they withdrew. Monyek smoothed his brown silk tie and waited for Lusia Taft.

Henrietta Feingold rose to her feet and announced, "I'm not going. I'm waiting here for Arlette!"

"But Mrs. Feingold, really, there's nothing to worry about." Mr. Zucker, who depended on the good will of Hirshel Feingold for his living, immediately renewed his coaxing. "Nothing has happened!"

Hirshel bustled the company out between the tables and ran on ahead of them up the esplanade, his hands churning at his sides. After him Mr. Zucker hurried to give his arm to Henrietta, who rose obediently to follow her husband. It was evident that Mr. Zucker was torn between his desire to run loyally side by side with Hirshel Feingold and his duty to slow down to the limping pace of Henrietta, who kept turning her head back in the effort to locate Arlette.

Mrs. Honiger, a cordial guide, sailed like a pink ship beside the embarrassed, slightly charred figure of Marek Harari. Lusia threw her pencil back into the belly of her purse, and Gusta Harari closed her own purse on Lusia's note with a sharp click. Gusta, in her old travelling costume, hurried after Mr. Honiger, who thrust out his head in order to emphasize the carefree vacation air proclaimed by his checkered cap. And the last to leave were Monyek Heller and Lusia Taft, who brought up the rear of the little procession.

As if taking shelter under the shade of Hella Honiger's bosom, Marek Harari hurried behind the limping Henrietta and the halting Mr. Zucker. His narrow forehead wrinkled up, giving his whole figure a questioning air. "I hope there won't be any problems," he said.

Mrs. Honiger gestured with both hands toward him and began encouragingly, "But Marek, everything will be alright. You'll arrive in time. You'll take off in time. And this evening you'll be at home already." Her bosom forged ahead like a scout in front of the troops.

"Yes, yes," Mr. Harari capitulated.

"It's good that you came for a little rest," said Staszek Honiger to Mrs. Harari behind them, pulling his checkered cap backward and forward on his head.

"Really, there are no words to thank . . . " said Gusta Harari, "It was all such an effort . . . "

"It's good that you came!" Mr. Honiger cut her short. "A wonderful opportunity to see the flat we bought here. *Nu*, so we achieved something in the end. If we'd stayed in Israel, who knows . . . " He looked a little pityingly at Marek Harari and returned the checkered cap to its proper position on his head.

Marek Harari looked down at the pavement, and the skin of his neck tightened. "I don't know how we'll go back to everyday life after this," he said, and his chin reached out to the ocean, distant at the bottom of the bluff. "It won't be easy. No, it won't be easy."

And Mrs. Honiger pursed her lips in annoyance and made no more efforts to cheer him up.

Lusia was tired of running back and forth, first from the hotel to the café, and now from the café to the restaurant. She tightened her grip on the purse beneath her bosom, dug her heels heavily into the pavement, and made an effort not to lag behind in the climb up the hill. Monyek smiled wryly, perhaps because of the fast pace which was quickening his breathing, and perhaps as a result of the debate taking place inside him. "It's all coincidence," he announced to Lusia, as if he were making a confession, "Why we landed here instead of somewhere else." He fumbled with his tie, and the square signet ring on his finger wandered to and fro. "In the beginning we wanted to get established, and afterward the children were already used to it."

"Yes, yes." Lusia swung her arms heavily and concentrated on the effort of walking.

"That's the way it is," continued Monyek. "A person doesn't always end up where he wants to." Lusia shrugged her shoulders and tightened her hold on her purse.

"If we start thinking about what we really wanted . . . " said Monyek, and groaned laughingly. After a moment he made a couple of bobbing movements with his head as a sign of cheerfulness, tucked his hand into Lusia's elbow, and said, "So what? We've still got a few good years in front of us, eh?"

Lusia's broad shoes beat the pavement heavily and she said, "As long as we've got our health. That's the most important thing." And she shifted her purse to her other hand.

The people strolling along the esplanade turned their heads to gaze after the cavalcade advancing between the calm oceanside villas and the bright signs of the delicatessen shops. At their head, the coconut trees emblazoned on Hirshel Feingold's shirt waved frantically to and fro. After them dragged the limping Henrietta, with Mr. Zucker bursting forward coaxingly. Bringing up the rear in sudden spurts were Hella Honiger's pinkness, Gusta Harari's little face, and Lusia Taft's stubborness.

When they reached the top of the bluff, next to the balcony of the Map of the World Observatory and the mast sticking out of it, Henrietta suddenly stopped. The cavalcade climbing behind her almost bumped into her like the ragged tail of a carnival dragon. "I can't go on!" she said firmly.

Hirshel, several paces ahead, came back at a run and kept on jumping from one foot to the other as if the sudden halt had not interrupted his run at all.

"I can't run any more!" Henrietta flung at him. Then she pulled her hand from Mr. Zucker's arm and dragged herself to the stone parapet of the esplanade. She leaned against the parapet and scanned the beach anxiously.

The unexpected halt cast the Hararis into confusion, and they initiated feverish consultations with the Honigers about the amount of time left before they had to catch their train.

Monyek and Lusia stood where they were, as if waiting for instructions.

From the other side of the bluff the German tourist group advanced on the observatory, and the echo of their laughter and loud voices rose in the street.

"I think we'll have to go," announced Marek Harari apologetically, pointing to the watch peeping out of his sleeve.

Gusta chimed in like an echo, "Otherwise we'll be late."

On the balcony of the observatory the war veterans crowded. They pushed toward the shell-shaped balustrade in order to examine the old Map of the World compass carved into the stone with its arrows and its famous pictures of towns. Peals of laughter accompanied their exultant shouts: "Hong Kong! New York! Berlin! Ja, ja, Berlin! Auch Düsseldorf!"

Hirshel Feingold skipped across the space between him and the Hararis and the coconut trees were uprooted in the storm. He shook the Hararis' hands rapidly. "Bon voyage! Bon voyage!" he cried, slapping Marek Harari on the arm. He capered up and down and announced, "I'm going on to tell them to expect us at the restaurant." He waved at the little group with a chubby hand, crying firmly to the Honigers, "You'll see the Hararis to the train and join us immediately, eh?" And, turning his head, he charged toward the observatory, where the veteran warriors were at that very moment emerging, accompanied by their wives. Hirshel waved the folded newspaper tucked beneath his arm at them in passing, as if to say, Yes, yes, that's me! And his short, colorful figure disappeared into the dense stream of tourists.

Gusta and Marek Harari made haste to make their farewells to Henrietta, and after them the Honigers, too, took their leave.

"I hope that nothing has happened to Arlette," Henrietta stared distractedly.

"Please, Mrs. Feingold," pleaded Mr. Zucker, in a louder voice than usual, in order to make his words heard above the vociferous conversations eddying around them like a current flowing past some small obstacle in its way.

"Don't forget to call," Lusia Taft thrust herself forward in the direction of the Hararis.

"The minute we arrive!" said Gusta, tapping her purse in response.

Monyek approached to say goodbye, but made place for Mr. Zucker who ran up to shake hands, bowing and making his brown hat bob up and down.

"*Nu*, good." Mr. Harari shook hands with Monyek Heller and Lusia Taft, who was standing on his right.

A moment of confusion ensued as the Hararis, ready to leave, were prevented from doing so by the organized group of German tourists blocking their way.

"Good luck for the future," said Gusta Harari in the meantime, and she and her husband nodded their heads in the direction of Monyek Heller and Lusia Taft.

Hella Honiger crossed the road with a confident air. Staszek hurried after her, calling out to the Hararis to follow them down the road disappearing between the buildings of the little oceanside town.

The esplanade emptied of the group of Germans, who started down the bluff in the direction of the row of cafés, and Hirshel, on the other side, had long ago been swallowed up behind the observatory. Mr. Zucker was unable to persuade Henrietta to continue walking to the restaurant, despite all his calming efforts and the brown hat nodding. He left her where she was, collapsing against the stone parapet, and stationed himself a couple of paces away like a bodyguard. His face was turned half to the esplanade and half to the ocean as if he were announcing a time-out.

Monyek Heller linked his arm in Lusia Taft's and took a few slow steps up the hill with her. Next to the observatory balcony he said, "*Nu*, in the meantime why don't we . . . " and he pointed to the two steps.

"Really, the beach is so big," said Lusia, clattering her shoes on the steps and approaching the balustrade.

"Yes," said Monyek.

Lusia leaned her elbows on the carved stone balustrade, between the miniature etching of the churches in Stockholm and the etching of Africans bathing in the sea in Cape Town. Monyek too rested his hand on the balustrade and read at random: "Shanghai."

"Tarnów we won't find here, and Tel Aviv didn't exist when they built the observatory," he said, and laughed lightly.

Lusia contemplated the mist covering the beach and the bay. Monyek fingered his signet ring limply, and after a moment he placed his hand over Lusia's between a picture of Brussels and one of Amsterdam.

"Yes," he said, as if continuing, "The main thing is that

we're here." And without waiting for an answer he added, "That's already a miracle."

Lusia nodded her head mechanically. "Yes, yes."

And she turned her head from the beach to the street. For a moment, she saw the regulars of La Promenade scattering to the four points of the compass—Hirshel Feingold bouncing like a colored ball where the arrow pointed in the direction of Moscow; the Honigers and the Hararis disappearing into the shadows of the street between the old hotels in the direction of Madagascar; Mr. Zucker standing guard on the latitude of São Paulo; and Henrietta frozen next to the parapet, her face turning toward some unknown point in the distance, a mask of anxiety.

"We can begin again too. Why not?" said Monyek. The words came out of his mouth at first with energy and in the end with bewilderment.

"Yes, yes." Lusia went on nodding her head, without remembering exactly what it was she was agreeing to.

Once more Monyek tucked his arm in hers and they descended the two steps from the observatory to the esplanade. And they set out again. Monyek Heller lifted his chin. Lusia Taft's heavy shoes clattered. Dutifully she breathed in the healthful air of the oceanside town.

PART II

One hundred million old francs, not bad, not bad! Good, good—Hirshel Feingold stampeded down the esplanade, and the pale, milky light bounced the reflection of the beach and the strings of brightly colored pennants on his green-lensed glasses. His forehead shone, and a little star of mirrored sunlight shimmered on his bald head. After bursting through the knot of German-speaking tourists, he took a large handkerchief out of the pocket of his Bermudas and with broad, swirling movements of his chubby hand passed it over his forehead, his cheeks, and down to the depths of his chest, between the open flaps of his shirt with its pattern of coconut trees.

One hundred million old francs, not bad at all. Yes, of course, I'll buy the Madonna, Italian quattrocento. I'll buy it . . . Ahh . . . Ahh . . . of course they'll open the gallery for me on a Sunday, for a hundred million they'll open anything.

It fetched a high price in the public auction in Cologne. Why not? Let Arlette have something else to inherit. Why not. Oy, shit, almost one o'clock. I didn't remember to tell them to get the Chateau-Lafite ready at the hotel. It's not worth a thing without Chateau-Lafite!

The rapid gait set Hirshel's face in motion. His cheeks quivered like soft bags and only the muttering which pursed his lips prevented them too from joining in the quivering of his cheeks. Again he had to pull out his handkerchief and wipe the sweat from his face. For a moment one side of his lenses caught the elegant houses on the oceanfront, the other side shimmered with the reflection of the bathing cabanas on the beach.

Yes, yes, I have to phone Rio de Janeiro and tell Goldwasser to invest in gold for the moment. Gold's the safest. Going up nicely, and it'll definitely go up more. Definitely. Yes, all the money from the sale only in gold. No, out of the question going to Hong Kong and Singapore with the heat they got there. What's the matter? Mendel can't manage on his own? No, not with the heat they got there. A bitch, this breathing. A person can't even take five steps any more without stopping. A bitch. Fisch said he fixed the meeting for the twenty-fourth at the Hotel Repose. Scholarships for children of survivors. I'll have to be there three days at least. Yes! And put the Hararis' son down on the scholarship list too. He's a survivor's son too, isn't he? Oy, shit, this breathing. I'll have to stop after all. It'll kill me yet. A plague!

Ahh, ahh, the ocean . . . I nearly forgot all about the ocean. Ahh . . . Ahh . . . *nu*, the air here's good for sure. You can't deny it. Maybe I should invest here in the Hotel Royal after all. They said it's got a garden three-quarters of an acre long. Out of the question to make it kosher. What an idea! Such nonsense . . . How much can something like that bring in today already? How many customers are left already? Ahh . . . they have to get hold of Chateau-Lafite. I have to tell them. How can a person live with such a breath . . . Ahh . . .

Even when he stopped, Hirshel remained balanced on his toes, like a sprinter, and when his legs resumed their running his body gushed forward.

One hundred million old francs, and breaking the bank! Ha . . . really not bad at all. And the article isn't bad either. With a picture, too. Arlette will have something to brag about. Yes, I left her a copy of the paper. He should definitely invest in gold for the moment, until he gets the license to buy. Fisch should put Goldwasser's nephew's name down on the list for the scholarships too. His brother in Israel is married to a Leinkram. Second cousin of the Antwerp Leinkrams in diamonds. Yes, Iziu's brother. I told him. I told him not to leave the block! Just when Krug's going past with his wolf-dogs. It was madness, Iziu! I have to tell him not to be in a hurry. And only in gold! I have to get in touch with Goldwasser immediately and tell him. And only safe.

Even if we lose something. The main thing is that it should be safe. We can afford safe investments now. Ahh . . . Ahh . . . Yes, yes, yes, not a bad idea at all to buy an oceanfront flat on the boulevard for Arlette, Yes, yes, why not. Let her be comfortable. The way she rides that horse Arlette. Better than her French friends! . . . Putterboitl's got a flat three buildings away. Also a good investment for the francs from Brussels. Oy, look at that . . . Look . . .

Hirshel turned his head for a moment to stare at a group of youngsters in beachwear. But his run was arrested chiefly by the provocative red color bouncing on the slender behind of one of the girls, who was leaning on the shoulder of a crew-cut youngster whose boots whipped the pavement.

Phew . . . just look at that! Everything she's got you can see, that little shiksa, Ahh . . . Ahh . . . phew . . . So what, Arlette could also buy herself her own horse. He'd wait for her in the stable. Why not. She doesn't look any worse than they do. Even better. There's no difference! Putterboitl's got a flat just three buildings away. Yes, they're all gone, the Putterboitls. All five brothers. Except Heshu, hiding by himself. They fixed their flat up not bad. Opposite the ocean. Just three buildings away. As long as Arlette's happy. Whatever she needs. Yes, yes. Phew . . . this breathing . . . a plague. Ahh . . . They really don't know how to live, those "Harari"-Bergers. What they look like! A real disgrace. As if they never even got out of the ghetto. Ahh . . . Ahh . . .

They probably still eat herring over there . . . Ahh . . . Ahh
. . . What do they earn already? Next to nothing . . . A real
disgrace . . .

Round the bend, the façade of the Hotel Excelsior came
into view, with the string of colored pennants fluttering in
front of it. A little driveway led up to the hotel entrance
from the esplanade, with trim lawns and flowerbeds spreading out from each side.

They have to get hold of Chateau-Lafite! I don't want
to hear anything else. Nobody should ever say that Hirshel
Feingold doesn't know how to celebrate! Ahh . . . The way I
entertained the director from the Jewish Agency. Not even
Herman from the J.N.F. in Belgium came close. The whole
of the Tour-d'Argent reserved for my guests, and all the
wines only from the 1924 vintage! Ahh . . . Ahh . . . Let him
invest it in gold, no question about it! I have to phone Rio
today. Only in gold . . .

Hirshel squeezed through the cars moving up the hotel
drive, ordering them with furious gestures to get out of his
way. He charged toward the entrance as if he were racing,
his breath coming in gasps, richocheting against the revolv-
ing door.

Yes, that Marek Berger, that "Harari." He was with us in
the DP camp. A sad sack then too. No fight in him. No life.
I better get Zucker to find out exactly what Berger knows
about those surplus iron deals I had with the Germans! He
never knew how to live. Why not, she can even buy a horse

if she likes. As long as she's happy. I have to get in touch with Goldwasser right away. By himself he'll never think of investing in gold now . . .

Good, good, very nice, let them open the door for me! They get paid for it. A mug like a *kapo* that doorman's got. Oy! It's after one already! Just don't let them make any trouble with the Chateau-Lafite!

"I want there should be bottles of Chateau-Lafite on the table!" Hirshel Feingold burst with a shout into the hotel's dimly lit restaurant, where a solitary couple was sitting secluded in a decorative niche.

"Chateau-Lafite, you hear. I want Chateau-Lafite with the meal!" Hirshel went on shouting even after he'd been surrounded by two waiters and the Maitre d', all trying to appease him with smiles and bobbing heads.

"I'll pay, I'll pay, but it must be Chateau-Lafite!"

"It's already taken care of, Monsieur Feingold," the Maitre d' folded himself into an obsequious bow, and after a moment straightened up, patted the sweating coconut trees on Hirshel's back, and pointed with a flourish to the table:

"Voilà, monsieur! They're already here. Four bottles from the famous vintage of 1924! It wasn't easy to find them but we spared no effort. We know . . . "

The Maitre d' concluded with raised eyebrows, underscored by a light laugh.

"Fantastic! Fantastic!" Hirshel rapidly pulled an untidy bundle of banknotes out of his trouser pocket and thrust them higgledy-piggledy into the hands of the Maitre d' and the outstretched hands of the two waiters.

"Fantastic!"

He walked complacently round the table, darting a suspicious glance at the pair of diners, who did not, after all, appear to constitute a possible source of danger. Then he stopped, his broad back slumped for a moment and only his short arms still stirred at the sides of his body as if astonished. The waiters and the Maitre d' waited in the dim recess next to the table covered by an orange cloth, crystal glasses, and the bayonet-sharp folds of stiff linen napkins. After a moment, all three bowed in embarrassment as a prelude to withdrawal, but at this point Hirshel raised his head again, looked fiercely at the Maitre d', and cried in a panic:

"My guests are already here, eh? They got here before me in a taxi and they're waiting in the garden?!"

The two waiters and the Maitre d' shook their heads in the negative. But Hirshel had already rushed between the restaurant tables, spun the heavy glass door violently round on its axis, and planted himself on the gravel terrace of the hotel garden at the edge of the lawn which stretched all the way down to the sand.

They're already arrived and they're waiting in the garden! Very good, Henrietta should always take a taxi. Let her go everywhere in a taxi! As long as she's got no complaints. Just as long as she's got no complaints. With Zucker I don't count the pennies. Last month I gave him fifty thousand old francs for his business . . . What heat. Only June and look how hot it is. No, no, the Hararis aren't supposed to be coming. They've already left. They said that Heineke was sick. Ahh . . . He didn't show up for the trial. It's always the same. Bastards. I'll still show them who'll have the last laugh! . . . What heat, it's a real scandal . . . Ahh . . . Ahh . . . The Honigers and Monyek with the lady he brought from Tel Aviv are waiting in the garden. Let them come to the table already!

But on all the hotel lawn, as also on the hazy beach, the colorful figures of Hella and Staszek Honiger were not to be seen, nor those of Monyek Heller and Lusia Taft, nor even of Henrietta and Mr. Zucker. And Hirshel suddenly stopped waving his hands.

They're not here! They won't come! All because of Henrietta. It was her who told them not to come. It's all because of her . . . But Monyek, why should Monyek do this to me, why? All Henrietta knows how to do is cry. That's all she can do, cry. A millstone round my neck, that woman. Crying and crying. Arlette's the only one who knows how to live. She's a treasure, that girl. Yes, yes, I'm going to buy it for her this afternoon! All she has to do is choose the color. And why does he look at me like that, that Marek Berger, that "Harari." Maybe he wanted to hint at something about the German surplus iron, and the dirt the British made out of it in the end. Another trial. Haven't they finished with it yet? Why don't they stop already. Enough! The way they looked at me, those croupiers in the casino, they were fit to burst . . . Ahh . . . Ahh . . .

Hirshel's breathing quickened and the drops of perspiration now flowed from the folds in his neck.

It was Henrietta who decided not to come. She told Monyek and Zucker that it was all off! All because of Henrietta! I'll phone! I'll go and phone now. Tell them to come straight away. They don't want to celebrate with me. All they know to do is exploit, only exploit. And once in a blue moon, when I want to be happy, they don't come. I have to call Goldwasser and tell him to invest in gold. It's past one already and they're not here. They decided not to come! I have to phone Goldwasser. Alone he won't know how to invest. I always have to tell him what to do; he can't make one move without me. He can't do a thing on his own. Always me. Me. Everything alone. Alone. Mama and Papa too and Belka with Zelig and the little ones, and Srulik. Otherwise he won't know to invest in gold as long as the rates haven't gone up, and afterwards put the profits back into circulation. I always have to do everything alone. Alone.

The strip of sand next to the ocean was crossed by a party of cantering riders. In the distance their colorful jackets gleamed, but the tiny figures themselves were only vaguely visible through the haze rising from the shimmering surface of the water.

Arlette! Arlette! She knows how to live, ahh!

Hirshel waved with both his hands. He rushed across the lawn and on hasty feet began trudging through the sand.

Here's Arlette! . . . Ahh . . . How that child rides! Yes, yes, definitely! We'll buy her the oceanfront flat on the boulevard. So she can ride and enjoy herself whenever she wants! She can afford it. This breathing is going to kill me. A plague!

A pack of dogs leaped out from behind the riders and bounded playfully across the beach toward the lawn. Hirshel stood still in the sand, and his legs didn't resume their running, not even after the dogs disappeared barking sharply in the wake of the riders and were quickly transformed into a blurred, dancing spot. Hirshel squashed his handkerchief into the folds of skin on his face. He took off his sunglasses and wiped the sweat from the wrinkles around his eyes and the sagging pouches of skin beneath. His feet were still quivering in the sand, the coconut trees on his shirt shuddered in a solitary storm on the vast beach, which was now empty and open.

Yes, yes, I'll buy her the flat on the oceanfront today. It wasn't her. Couldn't be. She would have stopped . . . It was Henrietta that told them not to come! It's all because of Henrietta. This breathing's going to kill me. A plague! Even Srulik. Even him . . . After the liberation! From weakness . . . a plague! I'll buy it. I'll buy it for her. I have to get in touch with Goldwasser immediately. A plague . . . Alone.

Everything alone. One hundred million old francs . . . Ahh . . . Ahh . . . Even Srulik. Alone. Always alone. This breathing's going to kill me. A plague . . . And from the interest he can cover all the damages . . . Ahh . . .

He stuck the sunglasses back on his face. For a moment the brightly colored coconut trees wavered in the lenses, but they were immediately effaced and behind the lenses appeared the pupils of Hirshel Feingold's eyes, and beneath them the quivering bags of skin.

PART III

"Can you still stand?" joked Monyek Heller, when they finally emerged from the Hotel Excelsior that afternoon.

"So much food, I'm not used to it any more," said Lusia Taft in a low voice.

They stood there for a moment, a few steps from the hotel entrance at the point where the path leading down to the beach split off from the esplanade.

"It's after five already. So late," said Monyek, and then added, "Soon our weekend will be over."

"Yes, soon be over," Lusia echoed.

"Over," repeated Monyek, and fell silent.

They turned onto the paved path along the beach. After a few steps Lusia said, "Oh, I really drank too much. We can't afford such silliness any more."

She smiled, bent over her purse, and opened its spring

clasp, but in the middle of exploring its depths, she withdrew her hand again and snapped it shut.

"Why not, why not, we only live once. A person should know how to enjoy himself a bit, no?" Monyek's voice rang out.

"That's true, really," replied Lusia.

Monyek drew himself up with a slightly dandyish air and smoothed his jacket.

"I've decided to transfer the business to the boys," he said, "I've had enough. Now it's their turn to work!"

"I'm not sure. After all, work keeps a person going. I like going to the shop," said Lusia.

"Everything has to come to an end sometime. A person has to enjoy himself too," Monyek said, and then added, "Maybe we should start collecting paintings, like Hirshel, eh? What do you say?" He laughed, and his sparse hair jiggled slightly.

"I'm not sure," said Lusia.

"When will we do it if not now?" Monyek asked again.

"Uh, huh," responded Lusia after a moment, without taking her eyes off the milky light shimmering over the water in the distance.

The sun had drawn a white veil of haze and clouds over its face and seemed to be standing still, without attempting to narrow the vast distance it still had to cross before reaching the horizon.

"It reminds me a bit of Tarnów here," said Lusia suddenly. "Perhaps it's the weather. The pastry shops. It's odd."

"Yes, it's odd," Monyek turned his head to the creases in his trousers.

"There was a chocolate shop opposite our house. Rozycki. Famous in the whole town," said Lusia. "We used to go with Mama and my sisters to buy chocolates every Thursday afternoon. Very good chocolates. Rozycki."

"Uh, huh," Monyek made a pecking motion of agreement.

"During the war people from the SS used to go there. They were very friendly with the owners of the shop. It was dangerous, opposite our house," said Lusia.

They had still hardly left the edge of the sand, no more than a few steps along the path leading down to the beach. And at this hour of the afternoon the expanse of sand stretching between them and the sea looked broader and more glittering than ever.

Monyek glanced at Lusia, who was staring straight in front of her without seeing anything.

"Yes, the past," he said.

"Suddenly it all came back. It's odd," said Lusia, looking ahead at the paved path and stepping firmly, " I really don't know what's gotten into me today. It must be because of the trip, and everything."

"Yes, well, that's the way it goes," said Monyek, and set off behind her. He fixed the knot in his tie and leaned over slightly, as if he were about to say something when they heard merry voices calling behind them.

"It's Mrs. Taft and Monyek Heller!"

"Yes, yes, it's them! They're walking too!"

Mr. and Mrs. Honiger were bearing down upon them rapidly from the bend in the path.

"So, you decided to take a little walk after the meal as well?" cried Staszek Honiger. He raised his checkered cap slightly, said "Mrs. Taft!" with a bow and a click of his heels, replaced the cap on his head, and continued with the same smile, "If we don't get rid of some of the food Hirshel succeeded in stuffing into us we'll finish our vacation with a heart attack, ha, ha, ha . . . "

And Mr. Honiger seized Monyek's elbow in a friendly grip, while Mrs. Honiger in her pink outfit bounced along next to Lusia.

"Hirshel went to buy that picture he was talking about, and Henrietta went back to the hotel in a taxi with Mr. Zucker," Hella Honiger reported.

"So what do you think of that Hirshel, eh?" asked Staszek, shaking his head.

"I don't know if I'd buy a picture like that, of a Madonna, I just don't know," said Mrs. Honiger vehemently.

"Nobody's offering you. In any case you haven't got enough money, ha, ha, ha . . . " Mr. Honiger squeezed Monyek's elbow.

"What do *you* think?" Mrs. Honiger turned to Lusia as if to settle the matter.

"Me? I don't know," Lusia laughed slightly, making an effort to keep up with the others.

"But that meal he gave us was something, eh? You've got to hand it to him!" said Staszek, the smile never leaving his rather horsey face for an instant.

The brisk pace set by the Honigers swept Monyek and Lusia along, and they quickened their steps. Staszek Honiger gave up the attempt to crowd onto the edge of the path with the others, and plodded strenuously through the sand.

"So what do you say, are you staying a few days longer?" he asked Monyek.

"No, I have to be back at the business tomorrow, and Mrs. Taft has to go back to Tel Aviv, for the time being . . . "

"Yes, yes," said Lusia.

"What are you saying?" cried Mr. Honiger. "Tomorrow already! What are you saying?!"

"But I haven't shown you the pictures of my grandchildren yet!" said Hella, quickly pulling an envelope out of her gleaming summer purse.

"This is my Claudia, a beauty, eh, isn't she a beauty? She's wonderful!" Mrs. Honiger thrust the snapshot into Lusia's right hand, so that she had to transfer her purse to her left.

"And this is Bernard," continued Mrs. Honiger.

"Yes, yes," Lusia nodded her head at the small images, dragging her feet in an effort to keep up with the brisk pace.

"Look, look, here they are skiing in Grindelwald." Mrs. Honiger exchanged the snapshot in Lusia's hand. "And here, yes, here it's with Marie-Hélène, my daughter-in-law, on the beach in St. Raphaël. Beautiful children, eh, aren't they beautiful? And here they are last summer in the Phillipines. They took a vacation in the east."

Suddenly Lusia stopped and gasped for breath.

"I have to stop a minute," she said.

Monyek immediately took her elbow.

"Yes, sure, we'll wait a bit," said Mrs. Honiger.

"There's no need," said Lusia.

"No problem. We'll wait a minute," insisted Hella.

But Lusia started off again, with Hella walking by her side.

"It's a shame about the Hararis," proclaimed Hella Honiger, "They work so hard. They can't even have a proper rest. You saw what they look like."

"Yes, yes," muttered Monyek to be polite.

And Lusia concentrated all her efforts on walking, her orthopedic shoes leaving a trail in the sand covering the path.

"What did they achieve after all these years. Eh?" said Staszek, wagging his long face solemnly at the beach, which looked very white in the afternoon light. He shook his head and blinked with worry. "Such a hard life they have there. Really terrible."

But a moment later he grapped Monyek's elbow with a laugh, and said, "At least there's no danger of the boys marrying shiksas there!" And Hella too burst into laughter, which shook the cloth of her suit like a gust of wind.

"*Nu*, good, you can't have everything," Monyek, too, smiled. And the four of them went on laughing for a moment, very heartily.

Just above them, on the pinnacle of the bluff rising from the shore, the balcony of the Map of the World Observatory towered. The sounds of traffic suddenly greeted their ears, together with snatches of conversations of people visiting the observatory.

Lusia stopped.

"One thing certain with us over here is that we travel a lot. We never stop wandering, eh?" Staszek Honiger kept on laughing, and took a few more steps without noticing that Lusia had stopped.

"Staszek!!" Mrs. Honiger thundered behind him bossily, "Wait for Mrs. Taft!"

Mr. Honiger turned his head and ran back with an apologetic smile.

"There's no need, no need," said Monyek, "We'll just wait here for a bit until Mrs. Taft has a rest."

"No problem," Mr. Honiger interrupted him.

"We'll wait with you!" Mrs. Honiger planted herself like a wall between Lusia and the ocean.

"Really, don't hold yourselves up," said Monyek. "In any case we intended to stay on the beach a little longer. Don't hold yourselves up."

"Actually, we told the Putterboitls that we'd be at La Promenade this afternoon. So really maybe . . ." said Mrs. Honiger.

"Good, so we'll wait for you at La Promenade, you'll be there!" Staszek Honiger exclaimed.

"Yes, yes," Monyek Heller and Lusia Taft replied together.

"*Nu*, so we'll see you later, right?" Mr. Honiger doffed his checkered cap, and crying "Mrs. Taft!" he seized Lusia's slightly swollen hand and planted a kiss upon its back.

"It's really a shame you came for such a short time . . ." added Mrs. Honiger.

"You have to bring Mrs. Taft back again, you hear?" Mr. Honiger laughed as he shook Monyek's hand.

"Yes, yes, we'll be glad to see you," Hella Honiger straightened up and turned away in pursuit of her husband's checkered cap.

"See you later at La Promenade!" Staszek Honiger turned his smiling face toward them and kept on waving as he set off up the path.

"Yes, yes," cried Monyek, signaling limply with his hand.

And Lusia nodded her head at them and for a moment

her curls caught fire in the rosy light of the sun which was beginning to set.

"Nice people, the Honigers," she said after they'd retreated a little way up the path.

"Yes, nice people," said Monyek.

"Mrs. Honiger said she's from Chrzanów. I should've asked her if she knows Celina, my late husband's sister-in-law. My husband was from Chrzanów too," said Lusia, and after a moment she added, "Really nice people."

"Mr. Honiger's got a heart condition. A few years already," said Monyek. "Since then they stay here all summer nearly every year."

The tapping of the Honiger's footsteps disappeared down the path, and they now looked like two spots floating and bouncing above the sand.

"Why don't we sit down on the bench and rest a little," said Monyek.

"There's no need. I'll just stand here for a minute," Lusia smiled faintly, shaking her head in a kind of bewilderment.

They remained standing where they were on the paved path. Lusia bent over her purse, opened the clasp, and after a moment pulled out a crumpled handkerchief hemmed with a delicate, almost transparent, line of blue embroidery. She dabbed her nostrils and threw the handkerchief back into her purse. For a moment she went on examining its bulging depths, and then she snapped it shut, and patted her hair absentmindedly back into place. She stood still, her face turned toward the vast expanse of sand.

"You know, one hardly manages to rest from all the travelling, and then you have to start travelling again," said Monyek after a moment, his hands hanging on either side of his suit.

"It's quite all right. Really, thanks for everything," Lusia shifted her weight from one foot to the other, and now she could make out the grayish line of the sea through the waves of wind, white with sand.

"It's a pity we have to leave already," added Monyek, fixing the knot of his tie again.

"Really, it's a lovely place," said Lusia.

"The air here's good too. Good for your health," said Monyek.

"Very good for the health," said Lusia.

"Yes, yes," echoed Monyek, and leaned toward Lusia, stooping so low that his elegant jacket slipped off his shoulders and glinted in the light of the setting sun. But Lusia had already tucked her purse firmly under her arm and set off again with a resolute and purposeful tread.

"What's the time?" she asked, after walking for a while. "Really, it's hard for me to tell what time it is here. I've lost my sense of time completely."

"Soon it will be six already," Monyek thrust his hand sharply out of his cuff, exposing the face of his watch.

"Strange. It's so quiet here. I'm really not used to it," said Lusia.

"Strange that we're walking here together too, no?" said Monyek, and he tried to laugh.

Lusia smiled submissively, and a light breeze blowing from the sea caught in her hair.

"Good," announced Monyek, as if he were beginning a speech.

But his hand suddenly dropped in a round, flopping gesture, and again he laughed silently. And before he could straighten himself in order to begin again, a muffled, mechanical sound of hammering keys and hurdy-gurdy bellows reached their ears. The sound vanished momentarily beneath the veil of fine sand intensifying the pallor of the sun trapped in the haze, and then the gust of wind brought the hammering sound back to them. After a moment, when the flashing light dimmed, they saw next to the place where the brightly colored pennants had flown yesterday the merry-go-round which operated on Sunday afternoons for vacationers' entertainment.

Lusia suddenly smiled without thinking.

"Chopin," she said.

Then she opened her red-painted lips and emitted clumsy sounds.

"Ra ra ra, ra ra ra, ra ra ra . . . "

"Right, right," cried Monyek gaily, "Chopin. Chopin. Mazurka."

"Ra ra ra, ra ra ra, ra ra ra . . . " repeated Lusia emphatically, swinging her head in time to the melody.

"They're playing it especially for us, like a request," laughed Monyek, and he too moved his head, his brown silk tie jumping between the lapels of his jacket.

"Nice music," said Lusia, dismissing her own singing.

"Very nice," Monyek chimed in quickly, and he, too, fell silent.

Lusia quickened her pace slightly. Her shoes seemed to tap out the triple beat on the paved path, in a kind of exhiliration.

"Such a coincidence," she said.

On the merry-go-round the horses harnessed to their chariots pursued each other stubbornly. In one carriage, a lone girl in a sailor suit held on fiercely to the harness of her horse. The wooden manes waved in the mechanical round as if blown by the evening breeze. The volume of the music suddenly increased hurling its shrieking sounds into the haze.

"Our vacation will soon be over," said Monyek, too loudly, and after a moment he began again.

"Before we leave, I wanted to ask you if you've already thought it over."

"Pardon?" Lusia pulled her eyes away from the merry-go-round.

"I thought that we should think about the things we still have to arrange before we get married," said Monyek.

"Yes, yes. Of course," said Lusia, and nodded her head obediently.

"Yes," repeated Monyek, after a moment, as if to himself.

And for a moment the only sound to be heard was that of their footsteps, tapping out a stubborn accompaniment to the angelic tune ground out by the mechanical bellows.

Suddenly Lusia stumbled and twisted her ankle, and but for the tightness of the skirt constricting her limbs she would have fallen to the ground. Monyek quickly stretched out his hand and seized hold of her elbow. Lusia's purse slipped and fell onto the path with a quiet thud. Monyek bent down to pick up the purse which had fallen open and lay on the sand like a big bird with a broken wing.

Monyek handed the purse to Lusia and got ready to hold her again. She shut the clasp with a snap and began dragging her orthopedic shoes up the path.

"You really should look after yourself a bit better. You should rest," said Monyek, hurrying after her.

"Yes, yes," said Lusia to herself.

Her little face suddenly crumpled like a clenched rag, and her chin wobbled.

"I'm sorry. I'm really sorry," she said, and her pursed mouth gaped. Her brown eyes, hidden behind the quivering wrinkles of her cheeks, stared fixedly ahead.

"I . . . I really don't know," she mumbled.

"Mrs. Taft," Monyek flapped his matchstick arms in the fine woolen sleeves, "I . . . "

The gathering mist dulled the colors of the merry-go-round and the day seemed to solidify in the haze without continuing its slide into the ocean.

Monyek's hands gripped his tie.

"You really should rest," he said.

"Yes, yes. Perhaps," replied Lusia, her hand clutching her handkerchief.

"Why don't we sit down a while," said Monyek after a moment, "Over there, on the bench."

"Thank you," replied Lusia and bowed her head.

They plodded through the sand toward the bench, and for a moment their backs swayed, one toward the other. Monyek's jacket hung awry on his shoulders and Lusia's short body heaved with the exertion of trudging through the sand, like a wounded bird tottering and flapping its wings.

On the beach behind them the little pennants waved, and close to the waterline, which seemed to stretch into infinity, the ebbing tide froze under a blanket of white mist.

Monyek spread out his hand, indicating the bench, and said, "Here we are."

Lusia took a firmer grip on the purse under her arm and lifted her face.

"Yes, yes," she said.

She crushed the flimsy handkerchief, carefully straightened her skirt, and approached the bench in order to sit down.

BETWEEN TWO AND FOUR

Every day between two and four the little girl was left by herself. The first few moments of those two hours—hours that would soon freeze until the world returned, thawing into its normal course—were still taken up by the usual routine that followed the meal. The mother piled the dishes into the sink to wait for after their nap, and the father filled the little kitchen—already steeped in the smells of vegetable soup and pumpkin—with the aroma of a cheap cigar that mingled with steam from the kettle and vapors that rose from the water poured into his tea cup. But these moments of grace came to an end when the newspaper dropped onto the father's eyeglasses, and his snores were answered by the mother's mutterings and mumblings as she too dozed off, and a prolonged oppressive silence took hold of the house.

The sliding door closed behind her, and her room drowned in boredom. Sitting herself down on the prickly blanket that covered the sofa, she could not decide how to occupy herself. The smell of moth balls wafting from sweaters taken from the closet with the panic of the first rains nipped at her nostrils. When winter approached, the grey window always seemed terrified by a looming disaster. Now, the smell made the strangeness in the window even stranger. When she blinked her eyes shut, the window frame continued to float beneath her eyelids, a phosphorescent green that quickly turned to gold and was burned there, a sharp stain.

The only refuge was the balcony, whose tiles still held the warmth of the morning sun's rays. She poked her head through the iron railings, above wilting plants in asbestos pots. The new scene stamped on her sight brought with it the cooing of wild doves, air laden with the smell of mowed grass, and the top of a birch tree, pigeons hopping from its branches onto telephone wires. The waves of her breathing caressed her and the room's terror was dispelled from her lungs, replaced by an inexplicable joy that seeped into her throat until she almost cried out. Biting hard on a hunk of sweater she had stuffed in her mouth to stifle the scream, the girl deeply abandoned herself to the waves of happiness that flooded her chest and swept along with them random pictures drenched in pleasure.

But just as suddenly as she had freed herself from the grip of the room and the sofa, now something inside her decided that she had had enough. At once, she found herself in the midst of a string of hushed actions, intended first of all to open the sliding door to her room and guide it carefully back into place, and then to open the front door, which, despite the well-practiced pressure she put in every fraction of the handle's turn, and the spit she spread on the cold bolt of the lock, still made squeaking sounds that made her heart jump and the whole stairwell pound and spin. The last slam, and the smell of plaster and dust that filled the stairwell, gave an air of secret adventure to the freedom now galloping toward her.

It was cool in the courtyard. Now and then streaks of light broke through the clouds and rushed across her face. They would light up the wall of the house for a moment and then dissipate, leaving a patch of paled light on the limestone hills. Fallen leaves, earthworms, splintered ice-cream sticks, and cigarette stubs were scattered around the foot of the birch tree. She lay her hand on its naked trunk, but weak with joy she could not bring herself to climb it. For that she would have to take off her shoes and the woolen socks her mother had folded down, and fuss with the folds of her skirt that flapped between her knees. Finally, the sun's warmth pulled her legs out from under her, and she sat cross-legged, spreading her skirt over clods of earth. She stared at the vein of a yellowing leaf until it became blurry. But after a moment, eyes that had refused to blink so as not to miss a single detail of the intoxicating sights were stabbed with a sharp pain. Or maybe it was the smell of manure rising from the sacks of the gardener who was then approaching the tool shed that swept the girl away from her reveries.

The gardener's heavy boots thudded on the stones that paved the path between the tall blades of grass. He wore coarse blue work clothes, his shirt carelessly tucked into his belt, black rubber baskets filled with gardening tools on his back. His dark face shone with a gentle kind of gaze that only deepened the darkness of his curls and mustache.

Whenever he rode down the garden paths on his rusty bicycle, he would fix his dark smile and black eyes upon her. Slow and quiet. When she lagged downcast behind the bigger children, the gardener, popping up suddenly behind the bushes with his shears, was like a wave of warmth softening the moment's stings. It was clear to her that the warmth was directed at her, the smile at her, and that he passed through the corner of the garden only to look at her. She tried to look pretty. Not to run around. To keep her skirt from blowing up. She was afraid that the other children would notice the gardener's glances. Without anyone saying so, it was clear to her that the looks would then stop. That the warmth would immediately cool. That it was forbidden.

So after what was to happen, on days when she would be woken by the noise of the lawn mower, or when the stunning smell of mounds of mowed grass would get tangled between her legs on her way home, she would take the long way, roundabout the building, so as to avoid the tool shed and the glance of the gardener darkening the doorway.

But now, when the gardener approached, her body was

so weak that she could not get up and leave, or turn her head, or even lift her lingering gaze from the figure clad in coarse blue, advancing with measured tread between the flowering shrubs. Even when it became clear that the gardener was coming straight toward her, she could not turn her eyes away.

When he stopped, her eyes were glued to his belt. The bottom of his shirt rose and fell over it as he breathed.

"How much do you weigh?"

The thick silence in which she was stuck was shattered by the gardener's voice, a rough voice, like that of a man who has for some time not moved his tongue. She shrank back slightly and tried to hide her body with a hesitant smile.

"How much do you weigh?"

This time the heavy smile returned to the gardener's eyes, and they shown with a soft, dark, warmth. In vain, she tried to remember the scale covered with glossy oilcloth in the nurse's room. The pictures evaporated even before they were formed.

"Do you want me to weigh you?"

Now the gardener's gaze lay gently on the nape of her neck, as if he were rolling her on the lawn against her will. She drew her legs under the outspread skirt. Clods scratched her knees, and small, hard bits brushed into her socks. When she stood beside the gardener, she took care to straighten her skirt. And for some reason the grass, the few flowering shrubs trying to grow between the foam of the laundry water and the puddles of sewage—and the tree receding into the distance—all of them seemed to be taking leave of her with great ceremony. But because of her weakness, she could not cough up the lump of unease that stuck in her throat.

She had never before entered the tool shed. Even its outsides were no more than a vague memory of her slipping past its door. Now she suddenly found herself inside it, surrounded by darkness, and the smell of soil mixed with the stench of mouse droppings made her knees even weaker than before.

"Wait here, I'll put on the light."

The iron door slowly creaked closed. In the darkness she heard only the sounds of boards banging and slats snapping; no doubt they blocked the gardener on his way to the fuse box on the opposite wall. The nearly pitch-black shed was filled with broken furniture, cement planters, and tattered books. More light filtered in past the sandbags left on the windows since the last war than came from the painted blue bulb that spewed shadows from its depths. It never occurred to her to ask where the scales were, or why. And even if she had tried to ask, the hard lump in her throat would have stifled the syllables. Still, despite the dark, she felt she had to be good, the way she always felt when the gardener passed by. She found it hard to rouse her body from its languor, but tried nevertheless to stretch her limbs.

Straining to keep her eyes open, she saw nothing but dark shapeless lumps. The stench, the darkness, and the snapping sounds swelled about her until she very nearly stumbled. She clenched her fists.

Cracking wood carried the gardener's steps from the other side of the shed. She smiled her good-girl smile in the dark, so that it would be all over and he would continue on his way on his bicycle.

"I'll lift you onto the scale."

A cold touch under her skirt, and she was lifted from the ground. Her limp legs seemed detatched from her body, and her head drooped. The gardener's grip enclosed her, holding her tightly to himself. A coarse chill sent a shudder through her spine and her curls.

"Soon I'll know how much you weigh."

The gardener hummed.

" . . . how much you weigh."

He bent himself above her head, again.

She still smiled the good-girl smile fixed on her lips. In the gardener's strong hands, her body seemed to have already floated away and abandoned her. Only the chill remained.

Somehow, she did not collapse when the gardener put her back on the ground and her legs, not his hands, bore her weight. The smell of mouse droppings and putrid rubber slapped her, like a sudden wave. For a moment, she stood still in the dark with the smile still fixed on her face.

"Would you like to know how much you weigh?" She heard these words somewhere behind her when, like a wind-up doll, she suddenly began to run across the planks, the black rubber baskets, the rakes, and burst through the iron door which opened with a whine when she pushed it. In the sudden flood of afternoon light, the shrubs, the puddle of sewage, and the mouse holes were blind to her. She gasped, and the gulp of breath froze transparent and bottomless in her stomach. Her sight returned to her only on the second floor, next to the neighbor's door, which smelled as usual of frying burgers and radishes. With thunder in her heart that shook the whole stairwell, she took out her key hanging on a string around her neck. As she guided the trembling key to the keyhole, everything went dark again. It was as if all her body had emptied itself and flowed out through her eyes. Suddenly, without remembering exactly how, she found herself within the walls of her room.

The parents arose, and the home awoke, and the kitchen filled with the kettle's steam and the smell of squeezed oranges. Stern doors were abruptly thrown open, and the girl's room was overwhelmed by the clatter of pots slammed back into their places and by the father's cigarette-filled coughs. But on that day, the self-confident sounds that ordinarily melted the void in her stomach were shunted aside by a shivering that would not let her be.

The mother's calls hurried her into the kitchen. For a

moment longer she found refuge in the dimness of the hallway, and then she dropped onto her chair in the warmth and steam of the kitchen. She sat opposite a window that opened onto grey skies.

Even after the chocolate and orange juice she stuffed down her throat mixed their sweet and sour into a queasy mash, she went on pulling at her panties underneath the table. She gazed out far beyond the bare arms of the tree in the window, and her gaze was shattered only when the damp cloth wiped away the cake crumbs and drops of juice that trembled on the table top.

The little girl dragged herself unconsciously to the big, flung open window in the parents' room. A draught of air and the smell of mattresses soaked with strangeness and the sourness of cigarettes floated in and out.

The shouts of children rose up to the window and drifted down without disturbing her gaze, still entangled in the arms of the tree and the raindrops of denial.

ELIJAH'S SABBATH DAYS

Although Elijah returned to Jerusalem a few hours before sunset, he didn't get in touch with Hila before the Sabbath had begun. The sun was nearing the strip of haze above the ridge of buildings on the horizon; the bedspread on his couch was disappearing into the dark blue shades of its pattern, and he was still busy cleaning the dust that had accumulated during the week in his room which faced the valley. He quickly plumped the cushions on the couch, cleaned the sink, and gave thanks silently for the fact that the plants had survived without water until his return. As the west facing room settled into the deepening light, he hastily completed his washing up. And only when he emerged from the bathroom with his hair wet and combed did he feel some relief, as if the weight of the whole week had been lifted—his studies at the technical institute in Tel Aviv, his room in the south of that city, his textbooks and diagrams, and the jolting of the bus trip which had finally brought him back here again, at noon. When he turned to spread the white napkin, which served as the tablecloth, over the desk, he was struck by a ray of light piercing the curtains. He straightened up and quickly drew them open. Then he saw that the sun was already cutting through the red band above the rooftops, and in another moment it would sink behind the mountain.

He was late. In Hila's house they had already disconnected the telephone for the Sabbath.

From the low cupboard in the kitchen he removed two candles and the copper candlesticks. He could not go to dinner at her parents' house without letting them know beforehand, so he wouldn't be able to see Hila this evening. He hadn't even finished readying himself. And he was glad that he had not yet arranged to see her.

He prepared his meal carefully, laid the table, and once again felt how these acts calmed him, brought him closer to her world, which was perhaps out of his reach, but nevertheless existed.

When Elijah emerged from the little synagogue in the Orthodox quarter, where he always went in order to protect himself from the danger of running into one of his many acquaintances and their mocking looks, he thought he saw Hila's silhouette in the street, emerging from the valley on her way back with her father from the big synagogue. He couldn't have said with any certainty that it was really her. The headlights of a passing car illuminated the two receding figures for only a moment—the man in the hat with the slightly stooped back, and the girl's pulled-back brown hair. But in any case, the time had not yet come to speak to her. And he hurried up the stairs to his room, as if she were sitting at the table and waiting for him there.

Later the same evening Elijah left his room again and went to the Center for Modern Judaism to hear a lecture by the Diaspora scholar, Rabbi Stern, about apostasy and faith in contemporary Jewish thought. He didn't consider himself a real disciple of Rabbi Stern, but in an earlier time, when he still aspired to devote himself to the study of philosophy, he never missed any of the Rabbi's lectures given on his visits to Jerusalem.

It was hot in the wood-paneled auditorium, and the seats were mainly filled with organized Diaspora youth groups, who all burst out laughing at certain of the Rabbi's remarks, as if they were the jokes of a paid entertainer. Elijah tried hard to concentrate and follow the speaker's train of thought, the crosscurrents of ideas leading to opposing and contradictory conclusions, the controversies ensuing from certain of the hypotheses balanced against the superficial attempts to find compromise solutions, the retreat into general gloom, and within the darkness—the blazing trail of the speaker's comet, leading his audience beyond paradox to the power latent in us, yes! latent in spite of all the doubts!

Elijah was bathed in sweat, both because of the heat and because of his inability, that evening, to follow with his usual enthusiasm the Rabbi's arguments. He tried to concentrate on the speaker's face, his neatly trimmed and squared beard and his upper lip rapidly parting from the lower one leading into his pruned bush; and his thoughts whirled about without his being able to bring them into line with the flood of words. For a moment Hila's image floated before him and again he stared blankly at the wagging beard. Once he even joined unconsciously in the general burst of laughter, without noticing to which of the Rabbi's remarks it related.

At the exit in front of the steps Elijah stood on the marble plaza; his back bent like a slender branch in the air of the early summer night. The groups of listeners swept into the street chattering loudly and he lifted his head, as if he were listening to the warm touch of the air. For a moment he was tempted to approach Rabbi Stern and congratulate him as usual, but before taking the first step he changed his mind and stayed where he was.

In the street, Duvidel and Nehama, his friends from the youth movement, walked past. As always, Nehama's arm was linked in her husband's, who was no longer a clumsy, ginger-haired youth but a tall, solid man of substance. When they saw Elijah standing outside the Center of Modern Judaism, Nehama nudged Duvidel, and he proclaimed, "Look who's here!"

"Elijah, Elijah," Nehama chimed in.

Exactly as in the days of their youth, Elijah shrunk back in a panic like a slug whose tail had just been crushed; and there was an apologetic smile on his face.

"There's nothing to be surprised about," continued Duvidel, winking at Elijah, "Don't forget that philosophy was the love of Elijah's youth; and a man doesn't quickly abandon the crucible in which he was formed . . . "

When he saw Elijah shrinking into himself, an expression of pleasure crossed Duvidel's face, and he laid his hand authoritatively on his shoulder and continued in a familiar tone, "I heard you're finishing this year. Good luck!"

Nehama, with the kerchief bound securely round her head as an unequivocal symbol of her married status, shifted her weight from one hip to the other; and tucking her hand more firmly into her husband's arm said in a musical voice, "Why don't we ever see you?"

"You've lost touch with the old gang," complained Duvidel with affected regret.

Nehama said in an animated tone, without disguising her pity, "Why don't you come and have lunch with us tomorrow?"

"Thank you very much, but I've already been invited elsewhere . . . "

Elijah laughed nervously and recoiled in embarrassment again.

"Drop in some time, when you come for the Sabbath. Just give us a ring beforehand to let us know," concluded

Nehama; and as they moved off she stamped the cork soles of her sandals, as if she were trying to crush something on the pavement, and pressed her head into her husband's broad armpit. She didn't turn her head to look at Elijah left standing on the plaza, and her resentment against him grew, precisely because of the effort which it cost her not to do so.

That night Elijah walked for hours without finding peace of mind. He roamed further and further away from his neighborhood, without being able to rid himself of the sensation that the dark sky was tightly sealed over the town. He walked as far as the southern ridges, looking back upon the clusters of light and heavy patches of darkness, and still he felt no relief. He smiled to himself at the thought that perhaps the prayers of the inhabitants of the town welcoming the Sabbath were still wandering, like him, without ascending. A few of Rabbi Stern's words echoed in his head, but he was unable to follow the reasoning which would lead through hidden paths to the discovery of a new outlook. He walked along the trails disappearing into the valley and climbed the hill again. Twice he lost his way on the path on the dark hilltop. He retraced his steps along the deserted roads and at last he approached the first houses, lying on the slopes like dark spaces among the dense green bushes.

When he reached the shadowy, tree-lined street where Hila's house stood, he recovered his spirits a little. The stillness welling from the gardens of the narrow street arrested the vertigo of the sky between the mountain ridges. The whiteness of the jasmine penetrated the gentle breath of the other scents and touched Elijah. Next to her house he stopped for a moment—to clear his temples of the hammering of his footsteps—and rested his head on the hedge.

From where he stood in the street he couldn't tell if the dim light in the windows was coming from the interior rooms or if it was only the bulb left burning in the corridor after the automatic switch had turned off the rest of the lights. He wasn't used to looking at the house from the outside. He would only glance at it in passing as he left on Saturday night, carefully closing the front door behind him, while Hila's flute resumed its flight. And what if the light were still on in her room? And what if she were still reading the Rabbi's book which he'd given her as a gift? Even if the moon hadn't risen, the stars were shining tonight, and they would illuminate the room when she opened the blinds. And what would he say to her? He would be silent again, of course. And her brown hair . . .

His hand hung suspended between his body and the knob of the garden gate, and his fingers plucked at the silence in the street. But in the sleeping neighborhoods of Jerusalem on the eve of the Sabbath people do not rise from their beds or pass down the streets. And that night, too, nobody saw Elijah standing there, or moving from his place and walking away.

During the night Elijah traveled in sleep through contradictory scenes. When he arrived at the floating and covered dock he remembered that he had to wait there for the ship to pass. He made haste to look through the round porthole and saw the ship approaching soundlessly with its tall white masts. At that moment it exploded, without breaking the silence, and continued drifting to the left. He hurried to the left porthole of the dock to see the wreckage which should be coming into view at any minute—the big, proud pieces of what had once been a magnificent ship. But all that appeared before the porthole was a black beam, with a filthy rag trailing behind it.

He cried out—it's only half the ship!—enraged at having allowed the other half to slip out of sight, apparently to the right side of the dock. There, at the entrance to the canal sat the director, heavy-bodied and ginger-haired, who informed him that they'd received permission to close the canal for their own needs. He could look for himself if he liked—added the director—although in his humble opinion all that had entered there were a few insignificant remains.

He was too ashamed to go ahead and look, although he knew he'd never succeed in evading the inspectors who would not be long in calling him to account for his responsibility in all this.

After that, he was not sure if he'd really gotten out of bed in the dark, drawn the curtains, and gazed into the grayish apparition clinging to the window frame—because later on, when sitting with latecomers at a party in the room with arched windows, the same grey light stood in the frame.

Dawn must have begun to break over the valley, because the orb of red light rose rapidly and remained suspended far over the ridges in the east. After a moment it disappeared without a trace, and everything was shrouded in darkness again. He was astonished, and then it was explained to him that it was a common phenomenon in the moments preceding sunrise, and that it was not really the sun that he'd seen but only its potential light. Again and again the red sphere rose and flooded the east; and every time it disappeared, the darkness returned. The others, who were used to the sight, dismissed it with contempt. They didn't stop their discussion, only echoes of which reached his ears, for he couldn't take his eyes off the multiple suns re-emerging and rising to different heights above the mountains on the horizon. He still didn't know whether dawn had come, because the darkness kept returning as thickly as before.

One of these times when one of the suns rose, a ray of light, apparently owing to the lowness of its angle, penetrated a crevice in the valley. There it hit a little lake, whose waters glittered for a moment, flashing as brilliantly as a sapphire. In the light, the blue of the lake stood out very clearly as did the steep white banks enclosing it like a shell. The lake was surrounded by dense vegetation and further away it was already dark.

Although he didn't stop looking, he couldn't tell if the

sight revealed to him in the light of the chance ray came from the distant rift or from a creek in the mountain opposite; and a moment later the orb of light vanished, and everything faded into darkness.

Nobody in the room had paid any attention to what had been revealed through the windows, and thus nobody believed that the lake he described existed.

The visions accompanied Elijah throughout the morning prayers in the synagogue and his mind was distracted, too, from the reading of the Torah. Nevertheless, from time to time the warnings—"And if ye do not hearken unto me . . . And if in this ye do not hearken unto me . . . " broke into his thoughts, increasing his inability to concentrate.

The congregation stood and cried "Hazak," and Elijah jumped up quickly after them, his long prayer shawl making his figure seem even more tremulous and insubstantial. The beadle invited him to lift the Torah, and watched as he approached the lectern and raised the handles without much confidence into the air. He hastened after him, just in time to support the weight of the scroll collapsing in Elijah's hands, and hurried him to the bench behind the pulpit. All the rest was taken care of by others. The scroll was rolled up, bound and covered, and Elijah's fingers quietly embraced the velvet jacket separating him from the Torah.

On the way home, he avoided the members of the congregation who came up to shake his hand. The shimmering streets filled with festive, strolling groups, meeting in the sounds of Sabbath greetings and children's gleeful shouts. He shrank to the side of the pavement and tried to bypass those members greeting one another, unable to face the invitations to go home with one of the families for a Kiddush meal.

In Hila's street the little house stood enveloped in almond and peach trees. The windows were open, draped with curtains. Their pale folds shook with every breath of midday air. It was hard to tell whether the members of the household had returned from the service or if each of them had already settled in his corner, while Hila perhaps helped her mother set the table for the meal. He felt the touch of the heat on his skin, the air murmuring with insects. He gave thanks in his heart that he couldn't go in and sit down at the table with them without having let them know beforehand; he would thus be able to prepare himself better before he saw her.

Although he did his best to steal away unnoticed, his uncle's widow, who was standing at her window and watching her acquaintances pass by, as was her habit on the Sabbath when she didn't attend synagogue service, caught sight of him. Even from the top story she could see that Elijah was swaying on his feet, and despite her pangs of conscience at having so long neglected the duty of hospitality she owed her late husband's nephew, she was not sorry to see him disappearing. She rested her folded arms on the window sill and looked at the group of people now coming up the street and taking his place.

When he left his room again, it was nearly four o'clock in the afternoon. He stepped lightly up the street and turned into the road along the hilltop. On the westward slope, the sun beat down with all its might, but when the road turned and was swallowed up in the shaded alley to the east, the light suddenly softened and a bluish haze hovered between the houses. He remembered the images of light in the Rabbi's poems in the book he had given Hila, and with a feeling of relief he passed the shady gardens on the way to her house. The sun hasn't begun to set yet, he marveled, and the stone houses are already turning almost red.

When he knocked on the front door, Hila was sitting in the dining room. The rest of the family was in their rooms resting, and her two little brothers had gone out to their youth movement activities and would not return until after dark. There was a book lying open on the table, but her eyes had been caught by the trembling of the patterns of light filtering through the fruit trees in the windows of the dining alcove and onto the tablecloth. She was not expecting anyone, and she knew, too, that it would be a long time before her parents woke from their naps. She didn't think of Elijah. If he hadn't called on Friday, he surely had no intention of coming, and perhaps he hadn't even returned to Jerusalem for the Sabbath. His irregular visits had halted so long ago that she'd stopped looking forward to them, even if only for the sake of the curiosity they aroused in her. The shapes of light traveling across the tablecloth led her thoughts to the notes of the suite that she'd go back to playing after the end of the Sabbath, and to the transparent weaving of its passages.

The flow of music stopped and she went to the door, sure that it was one of her brothers' friends arriving too late to walk to the clubhouse with them. She cried out in astonishment—"Oh, oh, it's you"—when she saw Elijah's slender form stooped in the doorway—he too smiling in astonishment. She motioned for him to come in on tiptoe, and closed the dining room door behind them.

Hila poured plum juice into the crystal glasses and placed them with their blood-red shadows on the table-cloth, and Elijah had not yet uttered a word, only laughed from his place on the upholstered chair, and laughed again as if he were beside himself with excitement. Hila sat down opposite him, on the other side of the table, and asked what he had been doing with himself. After he hastily answered her, his replies still smothered in nervous laughter, she began telling him about her little brothers, and about the intertwining music of the suite for the flute which she was now learning.

She stood up, asked if he wanted another glass, and went to the refrigerator in the kitchen. Elijah swayed in his seat as if he were sailing toward a lonely island in the sea. He was careful not to disturb the currents leading toward it, endeavoring with all his might to set all the instruments inside him to correspond to the winds blowing there. So close was he to the isle of his yearning, that the certainty of its existence could no longer be taken from him. He lowered his eyes and his gaze caressed the tablecloth.

Hila placed a crystal dish of cookies next to the glass, and he was afraid that she was going to ask him about his life again, and then he would have to unfold his troubled world and disturb the calm of the still waters. His throat constricted, and he didn't take anything to eat or drink.

Hila suggested that they go for a walk. He was quick to agree and hurried after her down the corridor, careful not to knock anything over with his lanky limbs. When they shut the gate behind them, he recalled the rhyming lights in the Rabbi's poems, and thought that he hadn't yet asked her if she had read the book. But in the meantime they started walking, and the scent of the jasmine through the foliage was too heavy for him to formulate his question.

In the park, the rocks cast low, distant shadows, and the tips of the clumps of grass glittered. On the main road the traffic had already started up again, and it was only in the heart of the park that they could hear the rustling of the grass which bent as they walked. When the low sun peeked out, their slender shadows were surrounded by red light, and when it disappeared behind trees or housetops, the shadows of Hila and Elijah were blotted out.

There was no one in the park at this hour. The light faded rapidly. When they stopped once or twice between the crossing paths, Elijah's body was jolted and lurched forward. But he tremblingly returned his hand to its place, as if away from a rare flower whose transparent petals were so delicate they could be damaged by the hovering shadow of a butterfly's wing.

They left the park, and sat down on the low stone wall separating it from the street. He told her about his studies in Tel Aviv and the words came heavily and hollowly out of his mouth.

The street was suddenly filled with cinemagoers beginning to gather for the first show. Hila stood and said, "Soon the Sabbath will be over."

And she immediately began walking back.

In the street, the people going out to enjoy themselves crowded in front of the snack bars and made walking difficult. Elijah and Hila were forced to the edge of the road whenever a bus passed and emitted a jet of hot soot, but he was still sheltered by her presence in an island of calm. For a moment they walked with their shoulders touching, and the tremor which passed through Elijah's body lasted no more than a second. Then, something made Hila burst into a long, clear peal of laughter. He, too, joined in, and was rocked back to his place.

Hila hurried, so as not to keep her family waiting for the havdala ceremony and Elijah hurried behind her. When they reached the little street sheltered from the noise of the city by its gardens and trees darkening against the starry sky, he said without waiting to be asked that he would not come in now, but would first go to say the evening prayer.

He stayed outside next to the gate and waved to Hila hurrying up the steps, bathed in the light shining from the windows. His fingers accidentally came to rest on the gate's knob, and he closed it slowly. As he walked away, he thought he heard her voice, the beginning of the blessing. Then he was swallowed up in the darkness. He was no longer afraid of meeting any of his acquaintances—now he had a refuge from them, and all the way he took care not to emerge from the shadows of the gardens at the pavement's inner edge.

In his room, he groped toward the window in the dark and looked at the lights twinkling in the distance. And still he postponed his prayer. When he had finished and turned on the lamp, his eyes refused to adapt themselves to the light. Nevertheless, he went into the kitchen and reached into the cupboard to pull out the candles to join wick to wick. But it seemed to him that the paper package was empty. He took it out to examine its contents on the marble counter and found that he'd indeed used the last of the candles the night before, without leaving any for the havdala.

It was late, and Elijah began to pack his canvas case with the things he would take back with him to Tel Aviv the next day. In a separate bag he sorted out his textbooks and looked for the copybooks he would need in order to begin preparing for his exam. Finally he removed the napkin and sat down at his desk. He began to study the diagrams and tables of calculations. For a moment, it seemed to him that this time he would not be able to last until the end of the week. He bent down close to the lamp and his fingers hovered upon the desk, touching and not touching.

EVENING RIDE

She was leaving the house when twilight had already begun. The faint blue light of the setting sun filled the yard. A sudden break in the clouds cast shadows despite the lateness of the hour. In truth, she didn't really know how late it was. Since coming to the house she had gradually lost the habit of looking at her watch, and in the end she'd taken it off to protect it from the mop water and never put it on again. These days only the slowly changing light of the north country, almost forgotten during all these years, told her the time. Now, too, without knowing why, she suddenly left the house, dropping her work in the middle, as if compelled by the sun—which had emerged after a rainy summer day—to go out into the setting light.

She had to bend down under the wooden staircase in order to unlock the bicycle. Crouching behind the seat, her fingers groped for the lock. Many alien movements had erased from her hands the old habit of releasing the iron bolt in one easy motion.

From the neighbor's yard came the sound of raindrops, slipping from the bushes onto the paving stones of the garden. The smell of wet grass, too, and of cold. In their big bay window the table lamps were already glowing. But the soft light, framed by window plants and curtain edges, didn't pour out to join the radiance of the twilight. There was no one to be seen in the illuminated living room, nor in the garden, nor in the street into which she led the bicycle, both hands guiding the handlebars over the wild bushes which had grown up in the yard.

The movement of riding carried her swiftly through the streets of the little town. No one noticed her hushed passage past the lit windows. Her body swayed with the deep movements of turning the pedals. For a moment she forgot the thinness of her limbs, the illness. The wind beat against the nape of her neck and made her sparse hair fly. She abandoned herself entirely to the effort of keeping her balance.

Without paying attention she passed the last houses of the little town, already crossing the stretch of birch trees and lawns leading to the woods.

Suddenly she had an intense desire to look down and see the swans sailing on the lake below. She pedaled up the road, and a vague anxiety took hold of her. Who could guarantee that the swans were still sailing on the lake? After all that had passed. Who could guarantee that the lake was still there at the bottom of the slope?

But her fears were groundless. The artificial lake was there, and a few grey swans, too, were floating on the shallow water of its bed. The water looked almost black, perhaps because of the clouds, which had again begun to cover the already grey sky.

Next to the lake was a café. She rode past the hedge enclosing it. Painted iron tables stood on the lawn. But the playground—separated from the rest of the café by a low, red fence, and its swings, the playground where she used to come with her mother and her brothers—was not there. Tennis courts had taken its place. At this late hour there was no one sitting at the tables, and she hurried past the tennis courts. On the farthest one a white-clad couple was playing. For a moment the man interrupted chasing the rolling ball and contemplated the emaciated, untidy figure riding by.

The trees at the side of the road were dark because of the clouds, which hastened the descent of the night. The bicycle path was swallowed up in the road, and the speeding cars whistled past her, very near. The effort began to affect her breathing.

She reached the main road and no longer knew where to go. In her mind's eye the old sights came back clearly. The little town with its streets and crossroads, the pathways that led to the sea, and the bicycle paths descending the dunes between the rows of wire fences in the scrubby fields on the slopes.

Again the sun emerged from the clouds, very close to the horizon and the distant roofs. She continued along the main road to the beach knowing that she wouldn't take the shortcut past the place where the synagogue had stood. She only took care, as back then, not to get caught in the grooves of the tram-tracks.

Beyond the promenade the light was still abundant on the white sand dunes. She gripped the handlebars tightly and went down the path between the wire fences and the black bushes. The low-lying light ran over the water and twice chased her silhouette.

But I've already ridden past these very bushes. I was so happy then.

She could not understand any more why she'd returned to the empty house, which she was cleaning for herself. A sharp sense overtook her that death would come soon.

She didn't loosen her tight hold of the handlebars. The twilight, too, continued. There was no change in the steady dark blue of the sky. As she passed down the road between the trees, shadows struck her face.

In the little town the living rooms were already on display behind the big bay windows, alien lives illuminated by a warm light behind curtains and vases of flowers. Not a living soul passed in the streets through which she rode. Her body swayed with the movements of the pedals, rising and falling. Without thinking she went on silently riding. Back to the house.

JET LAG

He set out on a short business trip. Only a few days round-trip. The names of the distant cities written on his ticket were like points on a child's globe. Without lengthy good-byes, he parted from her early in the evening and hurried to the cab already waiting in the street. He didn't notice when he traveled down the hill and out of the city limits because he was busy studying his list of appointments; and he spent the long hours of the flight reading newspapers and tossing drowsily between mealtimes. In the round windows the sun rose, crossed the plane's path, and receded into the distance. The straining engines caught up with the retreating light.

When they landed all he had to do was turn the hands of his watch eight hours back, collect his luggage, and leave the airport. He jumped into a cab and showed the driver the address of the corporation whose building was already familiar to him from the little colored picture on the air-mail dispatched preceding his trip. On the way he looked at the palm trees planted along the bay and at the Latin faces of the passersby. And when they arrived at the foot of the glass tower, he was taken aback for a moment at the sight of the ramshackle mud houses around it.

On the top floor, the members of the board of directors were already waiting for him. They relieved him of his light suitcase and led him down the long corridor to the conference room.

During their negotiations that morning, significant progress was made in the preparation of the global contract. Lunch was served between the paragraph covering marketing and the paragraph covering payments. At two thirty, at the end of the conference, Nicola Gupetti, deputy manager of the sales department, smiling possessor of a thin, bristling mustache, took him in his car to the hotel where a room had been reserved.

As soon as the bellboy left the room, he opened the blinds. It was three o'clock in the afternoon. Down the shimmering street four dark-skinned women were walking, their soft shadows sinking into the pavement. On their heads they were carrying wicker baskets full of many colored fruits and herbs, and the echoes of their conversation had a special, musical ring. The warm air was saturated with the smell of the distant sea—on the map a blue stain climbing upside down, northward. He shaded his eyes with the back of his hand. For the first time he thought: three o'clock here, eleven o'clock at night over there. He drew the curtain, and went to lie down for a short rest before the meetings resumed in the afternoon. He had given up in advance any idea of exploring the city. His schedule was too crowded and he was flying back the next day in the afternoon. He took off his shoes and lay down in his clothes on the bedspread. For a moment he clung dizzily to the bed which went on slipping southward out of the hold of gravity's forces. Then he took up his papers to study the agreement formulated in the morning meetings.

At exactly quarter to five he descended to the lobby of the hotel. By then he had washed and changed into the fresh suit of clothes which he'd taken out of his bag. His wet hair gave off the foreign, sweetish smell of the hotel soap. The lobby was dark. The door, padded with green leather, was closed, and the curtains were drawn. Dark lampshades cast narrow circles of light. At thirteen minutes to five Gupetti came in, and smiled with the mustache that sat in a straight line on his upper lip. He followed Gupetti to the exit.

The glare in the street had softened since midday, but the light was still full and yellow.

"Don't forget that the shadows here fall to the south," Gupetti smiled, and his mustache stretched.

He stared at Gupetti uncomprehendingly.

"You see," continued Gupetti in his genial tone, "here at noon the sun is in the north, and at night, too, the stars are different."

On the top floor of the corporate tower they took their places in the purple armchairs among the little palms of the hothouse in the sky. In the smoked glass of the windows the sea clung to the edges of the horizon under the equator's line. The draft of the contract was drawn up to everyone's satisfaction and in accordance with the hopes he'd pinned on this trip. And when they descended in the elevator at the end of the conference, the lights were already on in the glass floors of the tower, and the imprint of its windows fell onto the mud huts clustering round its feet. Gupetti led him to a restaurant in one of the dark streets. But the fatigue of the past two days was having its effect, and he hardly ate anything. However, he drank to the dregs the fruit drink which startled him with its heady sweetness.

When he lay down in the big bed, he removed his watch and turned to switch off the lamp. Nine o'clock here, five in the morning there. He lay awake for a long time. Because of the heat, he left the window open. Through the slats of the blind soft sounds rose from the street, rocking his body as it strained after sleep. A noisy fly drew buzzing lines through the room. Just before he fell asleep the bed began to travel again, and he slid into the night with rhythmic jolts, far from the light of day rising at that moment in the corner of the world from which he'd come.

Just before dawn his sleep was interrupted. There was a pale, rosy light in the room. Outside, the distant throbbing continued. The warm air was full of soft scents. With sullen impatience he remembered the hours he'd still have to spend waiting here before cleaving his way back through the journey of light. The jet lag complicated his calculations, and he abandoned them halfway through. In the end he gave up and got out of bed. He opened the blinds to the column of light reddening between the buildings. The empty street was littered with leftover fruit and peels.

The padded dining room door was still shut. He turned toward the exit. The morning hours were at his disposal. The closing session of the business meeting would only begin at three o'clock.

The beach was white and empty. The sun glared. He sat down in the shade of one of the palm trees on the bay. A few shells were stuck together in a glittering lump. The light invaded the beach in splashing foam and poured out of it in streams of white bubbles. The little lump of crystals of light appeared between the currents and disappeared. Appeared and disappeared.

It was only eight thirty. More than anything else, he was thirsty.

He was swallowed up in the stream of people, in the shade of crowded stalls. At one of them he drank bitter fruit juice, and with the other people crowding the marketplace watched an old crone dancing, tracing convoluted circles on the ground. The shaking heads of the spectators magnified the movements, and their shrill cries pierced the rhythmic beat. Suddenly the dark face of a woman bent down close to him. Her face was oval, her features carved. Her full lips split in a thin gash, and in her eyes the irises arched as if in soft, white lakes. Between the stalls a smell of black-pipped bursting fruit rose into the air. He pushed away the hair which had fallen into his eyes.

At one fifty he returned to the hotel. On the way he stopped twice in the shady streets retreating from the sea in order to drink. He hadn't eaten since the morning. When he raised his hand to push open the hotel door, its shadow was dragged southward, toward the darkness in the direction of the Pole.

In his room the sheets were smooth, and there was a sweetish, foreign smell left behind by the chambermaid. He emptied the contents of his jacket pockets onto the little dressing table, under the mirror. He straightened out the crumpled airline ticket. He spread out the local banknotes, with the picture of a tower and avenues of palms against the background of the sea. He tucked the ticket into his passport, next to the exit visa in the name of Yehiel Nammi.

And only then he raised his eyes to the oval face bending forward in the mirror.

Later you quickly take the suitcase out of the cupboard and put shirts and used underpants in it. You pull the pajamas out from under the pillow. Without undoing the laces, you take off your shoes, and go into the bathroom. At eighteen minutes past two you descend the stairs to the gloom of the lobby. Above the counter the head of the reception clerk floats in a narrow circle of light. You wait restlessly. At two twenty, as agreed, Gupetti enters in the wake of a swift shaft of glaring light. He relieves you of the suitcase and is swallowed up in the circle of light next to the receptionist. Head to head, they settle the account with a clear ring of coins. At two thirty you leave behind him.

On the way you seek her through the car window among the women, leaving soft shadows in the afternoon glow. Not far from the beach Gupetti parks the car, and the two of you hurry through the swarming queues of the central post office to the telegram counter. You make a quick calculation, and write with the pen attached to the marble shelf: To Zipporah Nammi, returning tomorrow at six a.m. Yours, Yehiel. You wonder for a moment if the message will manage to get there in time, and hurry out of the crowd behind Gupetti.

On the twenty-fifth floor the president of the corporation meets you outside the elevator and greets you in his soft accent, full of whispers. He cups your hands in his broad palms. Gupetti follows you to the conference room, carrying your bag. In the smoked glass windows the town and bay revolve as if in a furnace. The secretary reads the contract out ceremoniously. You all sign. The doors are opened by waitresses whose muscular bodies exude the scent of herbs. You bite into colorful pieces of fruits. The juice bursting from the skins floods your tongue.

There are ninety minutes to go before you have to report to the airport. They don't want to deprive you of the time left. The director of the corporation gives you a friendly pat on the shoulder and leaves you in Gupetti's hands, as if he knows how eager you are to press your face once more to the window of his old car. You glide silently through glass stories of the building and land at the entrance. You hasten after Gupetti in the red light dripping with salty warmth, and cross to the opposite pavement as if it were the illuminated bank of a dark, yellowish river.

Gupetti guides the car through the avenues lined with palm trees rising up opposite the bays. Beneath you, the sea retreats from dark blue into orange. The rhythmic hum already familiar to you shakes the old springs of the seat. With both hands you hang onto the window frame. The pavements recede from warm orange into the red of the scattered peels. Women carry baskets of straw and fruit on their heads, gilding like tall torches. You examine their tender necks and their cheeks hollowed out like soft, carved wood, and for a moment or two it seems to you that you can decipher something in the way the palms of their hands are entwined in the straw. You sink back into the springs of your seat. Gupetti navigates from the old-fashioned dashboard without breaking the silence. At sunset he points to the glass of the corporate tower in the distance. At that moment a white light goes on in all its floors. He makes a u-turn. You're still busy watching the shadows walking in the darkness. The evening warmth is sweet. Your breath comes in gasps.

Gupetti stops at the side of the road. There are only a few minutes left. You try to catch up with him through the smoke and the flames as he climbs the crowded stone steps of the outdoor shrine. Both of you sink in the wax dripping from the candles. Your steps almost touch the dark bodies of the trembling singers close together on the stone. Their heavy sweat glistens. Next to you Gupetti falls to his knees. His cropped hair is on fire. You stand alone in the streaming flames and the deep, spreading song. At your feet her oval face clings to the stone. You bend down into the heat. Her parted lips move in soft, bright dampness. You wipe away the sweat wetting your eyelids.

You realize that you've made a mistake in calculating

the time difference in your telegram. It is already tomorrow morning there. Your face is still turned backward as your body trails behind Gupetti down the giant steps. In one swing the night sucks the car into darkness. The dawn light streaming over the mountains there snatches her dark face away from you.

Gupetti gives you one last friendly wave. He places the handle of the suitcase in your hand. His thin mustache gestures at you and disappears at the entrance to the gates. You dip your hand into your jacket pocket. Pull out the folder of documents. The border policeman stamps the exit visa next to your passport photo.

At eight thirty I strap myself into the safety belt and sink wearily back into the soft seat.

I wake for the first time when the plane turns sharply to the north, somewhere in the darkness over the ocean. The stewardesses have not yet finished packing up the serving trolleys. The lights have already been dimmed, and the few passengers are wrapping their bodies in the purple woolen blankets. They force themselves to fall into an irritable sleep, which will do nothing to refresh them in any case. Next to me the untouched meal turns cold. I stretch out my legs on the seats beside me. The iron capsule rocks us silently. A loud, monotonous roar pierces the night. Down below the zones of darkness change, and the sphere of night from which we've been detached goes on turning steadily.

When I wake up again a ruddy light breaks through the windows. I throw the blanket off my legs and press my face against the clear glass. Above the downy clouds the sun lags behind, gently bounding. Her oval face recedes with the last of the darkness.

Above the seats the red light goes on for the last time. The rest of the passengers sit straight up in their places. The stewardesses hurry past in their purple aprons. I silently grind my food. An unknown morning whitens and recoils from the windows.

When we land I move the hands of my watch eight hours forward. There is no one to meet me at the airport. Probably because of the mistake in the telegram. An official of the border police stamps the entrance visa in my passport.

At twenty past two Yehiel Nammi emerged with his light suitcase and walked over to the bus stop on the main road. Heavy clouds were hanging over the fields, and the traces of recent rain were still evident on the road. He put the suitcase down on the edge of the asphalt. Small bushes of ragwort were growing in the clods of earth between leftover lumps of cement. Their little leaves swayed.

At three fifty he walked into his house. In a few words he told her about finalizing the contract. About the rest he said nothing. He apologized and explained that he had to make up for the night's sleep he'd lost because of jet lag, and without even washing, sank into the big bed at four o'clock in the afternoon.

She closed the door behind him. The suitcase was sitting on the table in the living room. She opened the two locks, trying not to make a noise. Holding the sheaf of printed papers in her hand she opened the study door. The room, which had been shut up since his departure, had a heavy, bitter smell. She put the sheaf of papers down in the narrow circle of light on the desk. When she bent down she noticed a small colored picture printed on top of the sheets of paper, the picture of a tower and an avenue of palms on the shores of a bay.

Zipporah Nammi took the dirty underwear out of the bag, and buried her fingers between the folded shirts. The bag was empty. Still, she ran her hand through its long pocket, in case there was anything left. The waiting of these past days and nights had increased her wakefulness. In the next room he was rocked on their bed toward a distant night, and even later, in the evening, when she would finally collapse beneath the weight of her expectations, he would slip away from her sleep to a day in whose hours she had no place. She abandoned hope of catching up with the retreating darkness. Her wakefulness sharpened in a dense buzz.

A faint light came in from the windows. It looked as if it were going to start raining again.

THE END OF THE PYTHIA

Many years ago, before the seething land came to rest, in a remote district between high mountains, in a broad valley surrounded by cliffs—full of milling crowds, noisy trams, and hooting trains—lay the greatest entertainment empire which ever existed. The City Fathers had covered the swampy soil of the valley with earth and planks, and in the course of time its bed was stamped down by the feet of revelers, who made their way there through the desolate roads of the wilderness in a constant stream of tens of thousands. With their arrival they added new streets and neighborhoods to the town, and packed the rooms of the tall buildings until there was no room left. As in all cities, so too in the City of Joy, people filled the squares and the stairwells, besieged the passageways, and were quickly swallowed up in the tunnels of the underground trains. All this feverish life, however, was only set in motion by the powerful pistons of the Fun Fair. Its effects were felt even in the hidden corners of remote courtyards, and even the scurrying of the rats among the garbage bins was controlled by its rhythm. The amusement park was located in the heart of the metropolis, on a field spreading from horizon to horizon between the tall buildings, and the sky above it was constantly covered with smoke and fog.

There was nothing, it seemed, to upset the life of the City or cast a shadow over its revels, but for the ancient rule of the thousand-faced Pythia. In the midst of their pleasures, with the foam still spilling over their bellies and the bubbles of grease shining on their lips, those sentenced by the Pythia were executed and fell wallowing with half their lust assuaged. And the more halting and obscure her verdicts, the more swiftly the sentence was carried out. With one of her thousand faces the Pythia would visit the condemned man, and some said that with her hollow visage—the mirror-image of his dread—she would press her lips to his in a farewell kiss.

In vain the City dwellers tried to track down she-of-the-thousand-faces. Hot in pursuit of the skirt slipping provocatively around the corner, none of them suspected the wrinkled crone knitting baby's booties, in whose guise the Pythia had visited the reveler collapsing in the street. In the heart of the Fair, too, where the merry-making had just been cut short, it was unclear if the apparition rising above the column planted in the cracks of the steaming earth was a giant clay image of her figure, its head seething with pythons, or only a curious natural phenomenon, densely concentrating grains of sand and debris in the valley's core. Her priests, too, were swallowed up without a trace in the fumes and vapors. And since they were known for their low tricks, they may even have donned the glittering uniforms of the Fun Fair ushers and taken up position at the gates to collect the poll tax paid by all who entered there.

Even the Pleasure Tycoons, who exerted themselves tirelessly to improve the Fair—and pocketed most of its fabulous profits—didn't dare to oppose openly the Pythia's reign of terror. They clenched their teeth at the sight of every additional condemned man but held their tongues. And when the Elders spoke of the ancient Fair which had ruled the valley in bygone days, they bowed their heads submissively. At that time, too, a radiant light had blazed there, and drink and delight had flowed freely over the Fair's counters by day and by night. Until one night, when the quota of joy had been met, the flames of the Pythia's wrath descended upon the Fair, and burned it to a cinder. The valley had turned into a swamp, overgrown with weeds. Until the current City Fathers had come and covered the swampy ground with earth and planks.

But for the moment, the inhabitants of the metropolis, limp with joy, drowned their cares in drink in the Fair's pavilions, and availed themselves of the services of the Pythia's apparently harmless substitutes. And thus, even in the outer streets leading to the heart of joy, the Pythia's mechanical dolls stood and offered their favors to those who could no longer control their desire. As soon as a coin was inserted, the doll would roll her long-lashed china eyes, heave her mechanical breasts, and swinging an iron arm to the right and the left, emit a fortune.

The moment they passed the gates of the Fair, those who entered were lured by the tent of the fattest woman in the world. Long signs proclaiming the precise sum of her weight, enlarged pictures of her limbs with pythons coiled around them and even her gigantic panties were displayed for all to see. The slick huckster enflamed the passions of the passersby with rapturous cries. And his two underlings, sniggering boys with sweaty palms, collected the entrance fee, and from time to time, with whoops of glee, threw wet and dirty cloths at the faces of the emerging customers. And at the edge of the fairgrounds stood a long green hut, its doorway covered by a heavy curtain and its painted walls sunk in tall weeds. None of those stooping to emerge from the folds of the curtain would say a word about what had happened inside, but their eyes burned as fiercely as the eyes of a man who has seen his own death. It was rumored that it was from the roof of this green hut that the great fire which had destroyed the ancient Fair had begun. But in spite of the suspicion, only packs of dogs would charge the green walls, scratch the planks, and retreat defeated, whining, with the hair bristling on their backs.

Yes, only the dogs relentlessly pursued she-of-the-thousand-faces. They prowled the City in packs. Emaciated, sharp-clawed, growling. And some said that the souls of the Pythia's victims had been reincarnated in their bodies, and it was they who were seeking their revenge. Meanwhile, however, she-of-the-thousand-faces succeeded in cunningly distracting the wrath of her pursuers: the inhabitants of the City, drunk with lust for flesh and blood, would throw the dogs the lavish leftovers of their feasts. And the more the packs of dogs quarreled, the more the stalls where roasting sucking pigs revolved on spits—as well as butchers, slaughterhouses, and battle arenas—multiplied. And the remains of blood and charred fat cut black furrows through the grounds of the Fair.

The artisans of one of the City's suburbs and the guard of the nearby graveyard (which was full, of course, of the condemned) never imagined that there, too, the Pythia had organized a daily meal for the dogs. From behind a rubbish dump, a skinny old man would appear with a cloth cap pulled over his head and a tin tray in his hands piled with the decapitated heads of chickens. An invisible hand had borne them there from the slaughterhouse under the noses of the butchers in their blood and feather spotted aprons. Meanwhile the butchers rhythmically dragged the birds from their cages, pushed their necks into wooden holes, and brought their heavy cleavers down on them like the fists of God on the books of pardons. The dogs, with bloodshot eyes, bounded after the old man to the farthest end of the rubbish dump, tearing his rags with their teeth.

They pounced on the skull bones and bits of feathers, which slipped from the tray into their claws. And while the dogs devoured their rations and pulled their claws out of the blood-soaked earth, the harsh hand of the Pythia continued to reign undisturbed over the City of Joy.

Thus the life of the metropolis continued for many years, and the hearts of its inhabitants grew hardened to the sight of the condemned and their corpses piled up in the streets. The whining of the dogs, too, would have turned into a monotonous and routine accompaniment to the revelry and celebration, if disaster hadn't struck from an unexpected direction. For to tell the truth, the first cracks in the ancient power of she-of-the-thousand-faces appeared without a single battle being waged.

It occurred rather recently. The traffic of revelers streaming to the city grew beyond measure. Multitudes filled the roads by day and by night besieging the city gates. Pleasure pavilions opened one after the other. They contained facilities nowhere equaled for sophistication and ingenuity.

Among the pavilions that were opened, for example, was The Grand Gambling Pit. From the heights of its roof in all directions loudspeakers proclaimed it attractions, and on fight days and racing days tens of thousands of revelers streamed through its doors. Among its attractions was a cockpit for cock fights, and behind it the no less entertaining rat race, where the competitors scurried on skinny legs through courses fashioned like hills and castles, swam across miniature lakes, and jumped through fiery hoops—with the numbers of the betters burned into their backs. But the attraction to which the Pit owed most of its fame was the knife and blade course, where the customers could place their bets on one of thirty men positioned on the starting line dressed in nothing but a loin cloth. When the whistle blew, and goaded on by the prods of the wildly excited audience, the runners sprinted through a gauntlet of blades and iron rakes. They were refreshed with cold water by the attendants, and went on to the bayoneted tunnels at the end of which the head of the first runner disappeared, to the cheers of the onlookers, into the smoking cell at the end of the course. At the beginning, special zones were allotted in the Pit to games suitable for children and youths, but the youngsters quickly outdid the adults in their boldness. They filled all the pleasure courses with their irrepressible eagerness.

And on the paths of the fairground, under the chains of lanterns flickering in the gloom of the eternal fog, a band of dwarf musicians strolled. In their oversized jackets they looked like hangers which had escaped from a wardrobe. Their big heads hung over the necks of their violins, and they swayed between the legs of the people emerging from the stalls, leaving behind the piercing sweetness of old love songs.

And so it was that in the face of the rising, seething tide of revelry, the Pythia's chastisements made but a faint impression.

One last deadly weapon remained to she-of-the-thousand-faces. But the recent prosperity and level of sophistication which the City of Joy had attained neutralized this ancient arm as well. For a long time, no sooner was one of the revelers attacked by feelings of regret for even an almost insignificant trifle—no matter how slight—than the pangs of conscience would dig their teeth into him and bite so deeply that they threatened to finish him off within the space of a few days. Many hopes had been pinned on the work of a team of scientists who had developed a strain of animals (so far, small animals) with sterilized souls. But in the meantime, in order to solve pressing problems, and on the recommendation of the Patrons of the City, the Breast-Beaters Street was created. Warning posted up on the walls of all the Fair booths instructed all those afflicted with the first symptons of distress to hurry to this place.

The sound of weeping and the cries for mercy were audible in the surrounding streets. Green-capped attendants circulated among the waiting people, and, gripping him firmly under the armpits, conducted the next in line to the entrance of the street. In the street itself the doors and windows of the houses had been sealed shut, and all along its length, on a jutting stone ledge, sat the elected members of the Pardoning Board. They passed their time by rattling collecting tins for charity, gnawing crusts of bread, and shriek-ing with laughter. The next in line hesitantly approached the entrance to the street, casting stealthy looks right and left. The attendants removed the purse stuffed with pay-ment for the treatment hanging ready around his neck, and with one last push sent him in. The members of the Board, without stopping their chattering, looked him over cursorily, and without undue effort diagnosed the cause of his guilty conscience. Immediately, and in accordance with his sin—slander, gluttony, murder—a long tongue would grow out of his mouth and slide rapidly to the floor, almost crushing the members of the Board (who made haste to get out of the way huddling together like a startled centi-pede). Or his intestines, squirting juices and acids, would coil themselves around his body. Or knives and rifle-barrels would shoot out of his nails. He was speedily removed, and the next in line was thrust into the street by the atten-dants' practiced hands. The affected member would usually remain in its enlarged state for a while before returning to normal. The sight of the pardoned sauntering through the streets with their swollen members became a source of pride to the people of the City, a living proof of the triumph of progress.

So it was that in the face of such an unprecedented burst of revelry even the fabulous powers of the Pythia failed. The lists of the guilty grew longer and longer, but although she changed her face ceaselessly, the ancient form of her punishments could not keep up with the scope of the guilt. Sometimes she would pause exhausted to take a breath of air on one of the hills surrounding the City. She would pass a heavy hand over her brow and contemplate the valley obscured by fumes. But a moment later the dogs would encircle the old man crushing his hat between his hands, and she'd be obliged to change swiftly into another shape and escape at a run.

The anxious queue outside the green hut, too, grew shorter and shorter. There, behind the curtain, the person entering would hold out a hand, which detached itself from his shoulder and floated for a moment in a small space full of arms. At last, the tongue opposite him, underneath a pair of dull eyes would click, "Guilty. Guilty. Guilty." But now the revelers preferred other pavilions, and the call of the last of the fortune-telling booths, too, was losing its fascination.

And thus, one day at dusk, while the Fair continued to seethe with its usual commotion, the bulldozers dug foundations in a new suburb under one of the Pythia's bastions. Her stock of the thousand faces suddenly ran out, and at the very same moment, at the back of the fairgrounds, a pack of dogs succeeded in breaking through the walls of the old green hut.

For a moment the dogs recoiled from the dazzling light bursting through the planks, but they immediately recovered and ran howling after the fleeing figure. It was on top of the hill when the first, the boldest of the dogs, stuck his claws into her dress and dug them into her flesh. The smell of her loins sweating from flight momentarily dizzied the dogs. They stood on their hind legs and unthinkingly swallowed the chicken's heads flung into their jaws. Whining furiously, one dog then attacked his fellow, and they savaged each other with stiff tails.

The dogs spun around with rage when the heavy shadow of a big, dark-eyed bird circled above them. Then in one magnificent leap, they flew off in her wake with outstretched necks and wings and mauled her with their beaks. In the descending evening, the big dark bird came streaming down and flooded the earth with a black, bubbling river. Shrieking, the hawks then assailed one another, casting red, fast-moving shadows. They landed quickly in an avalanche of earth that covered the river with rocks. Bright flames rose from the rubble and illuminated for a moment the sunset sky. But the evening breezes quickly scattered the flame's tongue and only pink smoke remained to cover the cheeks of the clouds.

When the dogs dispersed at last with their tails between their legs, licking their snouts, the contents of the Pythia's purse were left strewn over the rubbish of the streets.

Around the broken comb and wilting rose the pearls from her necklace lay scattered. One of the pearls gleamed for a moment in the last of the dying light, and reflected, as in an inverted mirror, the jubilation of the City of Joy and its Immortal Pleasure Pavilions.

THE DANCE OF THE THINKER

It began in the days of the great disasters, when hopeless-
ness and despondency covered the land like manure and
brought forth blossoms of despair. There was nothing then
to strengthen the spirit of man. Only he, the thinker, rose
up like a lion to compose his dissertation on the subject of
despair. He discovered double meanings and hidden meanings in destruction, and his thoughts reached extraordinary
heights of subtlety. From early in the morning he scratched
his letters in tortuous lines, and when evening fell he swept
up the pieces of paper and stuck them, one on top of the
other, onto a tall spike.

The cries of lamentation of the afflicted beat against his
chamber door. But under his pen they were transformed
into profound words. At first they were the voices of strang-
ers, and later the cries of his father and mother, his wife and
his children—which in the end died down. One by one.

Then, when silence fell outside, his thoughts sailed onto
new seas. Heroically he crossed the waters, borne forth on

the sharpness of his sentences. Like delicate bridges they led him with admirable precision along the razor edge between abyss and extinction. And thus he, who had never learned to steer a boat, succeeded in pulling the ropes of the eternally billowing sail, balancing his body in a marvelous rhythm on the planks, as in a dance.

When after a while he raised his head, he no longer saw the shores from which he had sailed. The waves had carried him to other seas, opposite other shores, where people lived who did not know that the planks of his raft were the beams of ruined houses, and the cloth of his sail—the torn clothes of the dead.

When currents swept him toward one of those shores, the natives of the place would blow festive trumpets, hang lanterns of colored paper on the streets descending to the sea, and come out in their multitudes. For his part, he exerted himself to entertain the distant crowds. For after all it was for their sakes that he continued to polish the dance of his thoughts. From time to time he would improve it by adding an unexpected leap or a special glide. And when they, too, seemed insufficient to him, he would go so far in his innovations as to courageously tear a plank or two from the waves, or, in a burst of emotion, wave the rags of his sail.

And thus, between one movement and the next, tottering backward and forward, his meditations sang, "I am sadness, I am joy, I am perfect despair! Even if the sea dries up, even if the land is laid waste, I shall go on dancing, I shall go on gliding on high. I am the irrefutable argument!"

With increasing daring he would rise and bend, retreat and approach. With pure spirit his body ruled the waves. It seemed to him that he could hear the cries of admiration from the shores, "See what a man of spirit! He has striven with matter and prevailed! Man has never achieved such transcendence! A spiritual man! A hero of the spirit!"

But when the wind scattered the rags of his sail, and the last of the planks gave way to the churning waves, the portly body of the thinker fell into the water. He beat the waves with practiced gestures of despair. And thus, quivering with panic, he was swept back to shore.

A group of boys playing on the sand mistook him for a heavy sea beast with a man's head. Full of naughty tricks they prodded him with sticks and pushed him back into the waves. They did not stop until he almost drowned. When he escaped them at last, he kept on flapping his arms but did not succeed in taking off, and his legs, no longer used to walking, gave way beneath his weight. With teetering steps he approached the esplanade from which he could hear the sound of trumpets and cheering crowds. They must have congregated there to honor the dance—he hurried. But pushing his way under the colorful paper lanterns, he heard the weeping and lamentation of the stricken natives who had gathered there to accompany their dead. On the edges of the crowd drunks capered sardonically, throwing their hands backward and forward, aping the agony of the dying.

That night he dragged himself to an abandoned barn. And there, on the straw which shook with the thrashing of his limbs, he gnawed the bread thrown to him as a reward for his prancing.

When he woke up in the morning, his body was empty of motion. Hands outspread and body clumsy, he tried to renew the movement of his thoughts—one step here, one step there. But the foreign barn floor lacked the power of the planks of his own ruined town and the dance did not return to his feet. When he tried to leap, all they produced was a foolish kind of skip. A clownish, drunken caper.

RITES OF SPRING

The origins of this story stem from something I heard in my infancy, in those years which lie sunken beneath the roots of events, and which, when looked at in the burning light of reason, leave nothing but fine ash behind them. The incidents were related by two unfamiliar guests who turned up to share our family meal, and who, as well as I can remember, never visited our home again. Although the events were related on different occasions, and each guest was only vaguely aware of the other's existence, their tales were woven for some reason into a single shadow in my imagination. Perhaps because of this shadow, and it might well also be because of the dryness of my childhood landscapes—for years this was the only way I imagined the sight of a forest.

I shall not attempt a detailed reconstruction of the pictures their words first painted. I shall only try, as far as possible, to present the tangled voices of the two speakers without being able to guarantee that they have not been confused, here and there, in my memory.

At that time the newspapers were full of warnings to for-esters: the hot weather was endangering the ancient forests. Although the summer fires in the mountains had become routine in the island, this time the weather forecast warned of an exceptionally heavy heat wave, so that the villagers were not surprised when they saw flames on the horizon. And in the village, which was no more than a few houses scattered along the sides of the mountain path, the event stopped being the topic of the day the next morning when the wife of the village elder discovered her neighbors' grandson in her garden picking plums. Her shrieks about handing him over to the local police dispersed the remnants of the impression left by the fire of the evening before.

Some time had passed since the intensification of the old tickling inside Berenov's, the third floor neighbor's skin, but he was too busy to pay any attention to it. It was almost certainly only a transient annoyance which would soon pass. Nevertheless, when he noticed the first signs under his skin, he made certain attempts to change his habits. He began to eat more as if to nourish himself and the stirring inside him, but he still maintained the weekly routine which had not been disturbed for years. In the morning he would make himself coffee in the kitchen, at ten he would buy a round cinnamon cake from the cafeteria worker pushing her trol-ley through the offices, and at midday he would lunch in the staff cafeteria. On the Sabbath he would get up half an hour later, spread the halva he had purchased for this purpose on a slice of hallah bread, and wait for the kettle to boil in order to make a fresh brew of tea. Then he would sink back into the armchair made of green plastic strips, and read the weekend paper, or take down a book from his modest library—a classic novel, or a work about social and economic affairs.

At the beginning of the stirring, he also extended a special invitation to his nephew and his wife to have tea with him. He set the glasses out on the table the day before, and bought cookies by the kilo in the grocery store. His nephew came alone because his son had the measles, and his wife stayed at home to look after him. He drank his tea without touching the cookies, and after a short time he said he was sorry but he had to run. When Berenov washed the glasses at the sink, one of the saucers slipped out of his hands and broke. The next day he invited a clerk from his department, as well as the woman from the second floor—the one whose balcony was full of cactuses—so that he would not be left with the cookies if something untoward happened again, such as the clerk being obliged to leave early.

A month later, he received a return invitation from the clerk. He spent a long time getting dressed in front of his mirror, putting on a tie despite the discomfort, as well as the medal he had been awarded for his industriousness. At the clerk's house he was seated in the place of honor at the head of the table covered with yellow oilcloth, and served his tea before anyone else. But as he had feared, the tie prevented him from enjoying it. Moreover, as he was attempting to take his turn in contributing to the conversation by mentioning one of the names that kept on cropping up—each time in a different order—the tickling inside increased to such an extent that he almost burst out laughing.

But, in spite of these modest changes in his routine, who knows if he would have paid attention to the stirring under his skin without what happened one day on his way home from work.

That same evening the forest in the valley close to the village burned down. The first columns of smoke rose from the middle of the forest, and by the time the villagers arrived the whole heart of the valley was full of tall, dense flames. The ancient forest stretched from the outskirts of the village to beyond the mountain ridge. The tall tree trunks were sunk in heaps of needles, and when walking on them one slipped, shoes sunk into the rot. Darkness developed at the moment of entrance, and it made it seem as if one were carving a way through a wall of trees. Even the cries of a straying wild boar were returned from directions so unexpected that the boar itself took fright and lay down in surrender on the blanket of pine needles. Beams of light danced on the heaps of needles, and through the bird calls, insects' buzzing, and creaking tree trunks, the gurgling of the little stream could be heard. It gushed down in the brightness through the trees into rock-rimmed pools, where the vapors rose dizzily into the forest's chiaroscuro.

The forest and the stream were the villagers' pride. On holidays they would go out to the needle-covered clearings next to the stream, bury their bottles of wine and watermelons in its water, and at midday, after a freezing dip, they would take out their packages of bread and cheese and remove the chilled delicacies from their hiding places.

Life in the hilly villages of the island proceeded according to laws of its own, unintelligible to the waves of tourists from the mainland. Even when the time came for the young men to leave the courtyards with the drying sunflower seeds and lizards to hire themselves out in the cities of the mainland, they were not assimilated among the city dwellers. With their stern, heavy tread, they stood out on the boulevards, as if they had never stopped climbing the mountain paths. When they returned to the island, the empty rooms of the old people awaited them. Soon the memories of the mainland faded from their minds and were completely covered by the whispering of the forests and the sharp mountain air.

That evening the fire did not succeed in taking hold of the ancient trees and felling them at once. First it climbed along the bark to the branches, and only when the trunk was left bald and blazing did the tree move from its place and fall. The piles of needles were covered with flames as if with tender plants, and quickly collapsed.

From their elders the villagers knew there was nothing to be done when an ancient forest caught fire. They watched from a distance as the local firefighters dutifully passed water in a chain to the edges of the fire, but their full pails were not even enough to quench the smoldering embers.

On the initiative of the school teacher and his pupils, the villagers dug a ditch between the forest and the village. Over the shadowy row of workers evening fell, red and solemn. Sparks flew and heated the night sky. When they had finished, the diggers gathered with their tools at the top of the village and gazed at the burning valley which looked like a red city spreading over the mountain range: The last battles were still being waged between fire and stream, with the flames flaring up wildly over the stream's bed and dropping down again in roaring billows of black smoke.

The fire stopped at the edge of the forest even before reaching the ditch, as if it knew its appointed limits in advance and had no intention of overstepping them. Only the next afternoon did the black cloud slide over the valley to the sea, covering the window sills with a fine film of soot. The blue shutters of the houses stayed shut and a new, direct light whipped the courtyards.

That night's news broadcasts on the island began with the forest fire. The broadcaster announced that the experts forecast an ongoing wave of fires, and called on the population and the fire fighters not to give way to despair. At the end of the broadcast, he quoted the official version which blamed the outbreak of the fire on neglected embers of shepherds' fires.

Inside their houses, behind their closed shutters, the villagers dismissed the voice coming from the radio with a shrug of their shoulders. They gathered around the elders in silence and listened intently to their words.

When Berenov left the office he felt a burning in his throat, and recalled that he had already felt a burning that morning in exactly the same place. When he crossed the square he decided to go into the pharmacy. And when he took the medicine from the beefy pharmacist, with her too stiffly starched white gown, he felt an urgent need to relieve himself of the softness between his legs. He asked if he could go to the lavatory. The pharmacist looked him suspiciously up and down and said curtly that the place was not tidy. Berenov acquiesced in advance to the poor conditions, supposed that she was over-scrupulous, or that there was no toilet paper there. He took the key and trailed behind her to the door leading to the courtyard. There the pharmacist pointed to a structure stationed behind bunches of flowers for sale in olive tins.

Berenov groped for the lock with the key and went inside. He closed the window which was open to the courtyard and the flowers, holding his breath. In the narrow space he struggled with his briefcase, his hat, and his clothes. He placed the key, which was attached to a little loop of rope, on the concrete window sill. He squatted down and did his business with a feeling of relief, pulled the curving wire chain of the water tank, and a dirty stream burst into the hollow between the footholds. He took his briefcase, hanging miraculously on the door handle, and his hat suspended on the knob of the bolt, and turned to take the key. But as if under a spell cast by the pharmacist, the key slipped and fell. Berenov searched around his feet, but the key had fallen into the murky pool. Hoping to find it close to the rim, he groped with two fingers, but the key was not to be found. In dread of facing the pharmacist's look, he pushed his whole hand in and swept it to and fro. A dense, slippery lump pushed into his fingers. In the nausea which seized him he began to shiver, and he shook his fingers. He quickly slid his hand in deeper, close to the drain. His shirt got wet. He finally snatched the key, but there was a bit of paper sticking to the little loop of the rope. With his dry hand he kept hold of his hat and briefcase. He stepped out and locked the door with the wet key.

In the yard the flowers stood red and yellow in the tins. On the other side the pharmacy door was pockmarked and full of locks. He felt dizzy.

Berenov pushed the iron door open. In the back room big bottles stood in straw baskets, and two pharmacists bent over a table. In the corner he discovered a basin. He washed his hands with plenty of soap, and he also washed his shirt cuff. Then he washed the key and the little loop of rope and he trembled. He was afraid that the pharmacist would see that the key was wet, and he put it down without a word on the shelf under the cabinets holding the medicine. Drops formed around the key. The pharmacist took it and gave him a sharp look. He bowed his head in thanks, and went out.

In the square he was dazed by the noise and the light. The smell of grilled meat wafted from the steak shops, and people licked ice cream cones. With his dry hand he held his briefcase and hat, and he spread the fingers open on the other one. The skin of his arm under the wet cuff stung. Berenov almost stumbled.

The next day he did not go to work, nor did he go down to the grocery store to phone and let them know. For a long time he shuffled back and forth from the rusty basin in the bathroom to the kitchen sink, and he no longer knew if the slipperiness on his fingers was a coating of excrement or soap slime. Afterward he sat down in the armchair whose plastic strips were hollowed out in the shape of his back, and waited tensely for some time, until with a feeling of relief he noticed a sharp pinching in his chest.

He fixed his eyes on the corner of the ceiling where the walls met. Spiders scurried there on thin legs. On a normal day armed with a broom, he would probably have gone out to do battle with them from the top of the kitchen table, on which he would have stood the stool with the drawer where he kept shoe polish and brushes. But now he greeted the busy life on the ceiling with a certain pleasure.

The weight was concentrated in his chest. He stretched so that the folds of his body would not inhibit the stirring, and tried hurriedly to steal a breath in order not to tear anything with a too sharp movement of his ribs. In the end he dozed off with his limbs sprawling. A thin line of spittle trembled between two bubbles on his protruding lips.

When he woke up his body was drenched in sweat. The heaviness in his chest had intensified and even before he unbuttoned his shirt he knew that something unnatural had happened. And indeed, in the middle of his chest, from the head of a yellowish swelling, rose a stem topped with two elongated tiny leaves. The little stem trembled slightly at the touch of the edges of his shirt and sprang up straight. Around it on the expanse of his chest grey hairs fluttered and a few pimples were scattered between his nipples. His chest rose and fell, quivering slightly, and his breath flowed undisturbed.

After a moment the tickling began again in another spot. The area swelled and hardened quickly. And when Berenov blinked his eyes for a moment, a deep, zigzagging groove appeared in the growth. Immediately afterward a folded sprout pushed up from the slit, unsheathed its head from between two leaves, and stretched toward the ceiling.

A week later, a fierce, prolonged fire broke out on the island. This time the flames spread along the range to the chain of mountains in the south. For three days the fire raged, despite the efforts of the firefighters, whose brightly colored uniforms testified to the waves of different conquerors who had ruled the island. Their commander arrived from the mainland after two days, and furiously summoned help over the burnished telegraph instruments. But owing to the bad roads, the fire-engines—their bells tinkling as they drove—arrived only after the fire was over.

The next day the reporters arrived from the mainland, and on the same plane a geological research team and reinforcements of high-ranking officers. The reporters settled down in the inn improvised in one of the village houses and took down the words of the sweating fire-brigade commander. But their efforts to make the villagers talk were in vain. The doors of the houses were locked, and their blue shutters remained closed all day long. With no one to gather their petals, the rose bushes bloomed in the sun-whipped gardens and there was not a soul to be seen next to the bougainvillea hedges nor under the wasp-covered mulberry trees. When the reporters finally succeeded in cornering the old man in whose house they were staying—on his way out into the yard to relieve himself—he gazed vaguely at their loud attire and finally mumbled, "It should have come a long time ago. Yes. Yes. A long time ago."

The growth on Berenov's chest advanced steadily. First the stems rose to the height of a lawn, and then some of them burst forth and branched out. His body burned in a fever of burgeoning growth. The rest of the activities of his life slowed, almost coming to a standstill.

It must have been after two or three days that he decided he had to wash himself. By supporting himself with both hands on the back of the armchair, and thrusting the upper half of his body forward, he began his journey to the bathroom. Still wondering at the strength of his arms, he straightened up and stood on his feet. On the way he panted for breath, and leaned on the furniture in front of him. He crossed the dark passage and fell with outstretched hands on the frame of the bathroom door. He gripped the iron basin, and when he got his breath back, the sight of a hollow-cheeked face with a slight greenish tinge, flashed back at him from the mirror.

After a blur of time (now a number of actions of different duration slipped from Berenov's memory, so that he skipped from situation to situation without any clear idea of what had happened between them) the iron bath was full, and he found himself sunk in it up to his chin. The film on top of the water was torn by branches, while on either side of the tub supple grasses spread, trembling in the water. When he pushed his feet against the bottom of the bath, he could slide on the moss covering his back, and he was grateful for the intelligence of the growth which had not concentrated all its might on his back, and thus did not make it excessively difficult for him to lie down.

He had never dried himself so carefully in his life. Branch after branch was honored by a toweling. He was especially careful in blotting the water from his feet. Sitting on the edge of the bath, leaning slightly forward, he did not skip a single patch of green between his toes.

Getting dressed was difficult. He gave up the idea of putting on his underclothes, and when he pushed his legs into the cloth cylinders of his trousers he was careful not to harm the branches. Owing to the concentrated growth in his armpits and on the muscles of his chest, he had to exert himself to get his arms into his shirt sleeves. During one of his clumsy attempts, his muscles betrayed him, and his arm knocked stiffly against his chest. A stream of vapors burst from the crushed branches. His head spun, and he fell to the floor.

When he came to, the bathroom was full of warm liquids. Berenov felt faint again. When he recovered his strength, he moved his body and started back to the room. On the way he fainted again for an unclear length of time. With a final effort, whose details were vague to him, he lifted his body and sank between the arms of the green plastic chair.

Everyone waited for the next fire as for a decisive battle. The jewel of the firefighter's preparations was the small yellow plane ready on the shore next to the hut with the wireless equipment. When the alarm sounded, the plane was supposed to fill the container bulging from its belly with seawater, and in a quick flight to the mountains empty the water onto the flames. For the last few days the yellow plane and its pilot had been a magnet attracting the children of recent immigrants who lived on the coastal strip. In the villages, however, high on the mountain roads, the news of the plane was received with indifference. Although there, too, everyone was waiting for the return of the flames.

The fire broke out unexpectedly on the northern range. It seemed that the tongues of flame were mocking the firefighters by advancing underground toward unexpected places. Soon the flames were visible in the distance, and immediately afterward the sight was also confirmed by the state of the art instruments, which went on ticking and registering as they were dragged to the fire.

This time a large crowd gathered. The geologists stationed themselves next to their measuring tools. The new settlers hastened up the mountainside, but owing to their inexperience they ran most of the way and reached the ridge out of breath. The fire brigade officers with bristling mustaches paraded among the crowd, and waited for the airplane. The last to arrive were the reporters who took up their places in the first row, close to the flames' frontier.

The plane crossed the line of the ridge. Its yellow belly glittered in the sun and sprayed a trail of water behind it.

In front of the fire zone, which had spread to the valleys in the meantime, the plane circled once and once again, waved its wings at the spectators, and then leaped toward the flames.

The plane's container opened its flaps as planned and dropped a heavy column of water. But the tongues of fire, which shrank for a moment, leaped up again more fiercely than ever, and almost licked the flaps of the container. The plane, relieved of its weight, rocked, and the water sprayed wildly around it. The waves of heat buffeted it as if it were a kite whose strings had become entangled. And in the end it turned it over, with its nose pointing to the ground. With water still pouring from its yellow wings, the plane sank swiftly into the flames.

The fire stopped raging four days later, and only when the piles of smoldering embers in the area cooled were the rescue teams and the reporters able to go out to look for the plane's wreckage. But to their disappointment, the little plane and its pilot had disappeared, as if the whole commotion had nothing to do with them at all.

At the same time the geologists continued their measurements along the coastal strip, followed by an ever lengthening trail of immigrants, who had begun to discover disturbing signs in their fields facing the sea. After a week of observations the geologists were able to confirm their suspicions. But the rumor that the island was sinking had already spread even before they published their findings. The immigrants, who had despairingly watched their fields being covered with seawater, hurried to pack their bundles—well-trained in wandering—and did not wait for explanations. The researchers turned to the reporters and informed them emotionally that everything indicated the presence of a rare phenomenon, hitherto known only in theory, of the rapid sinking of longitudinal folds which foretold, without the shadow of a doubt, the beginning of the era of the great sinking of the crust of the earth . . . Hot on the heels of the reporters the geologists, too, quickly folded up their measuring instruments, and on the narrow road on the way to the airport they were already mingling with a stream of immigrants, tourists, and government officials, all escaping as fast as they could from the sinking island.

The little airport, usually so sluggish, was humming with rescue planes which had arrived from the mainland. In the waiting hall the counters of the single kiosk had long been emptied, and people elbowed their way to the exit without standing on dignity. In the hubbub of desertion, nobody paid any attention to the young men who alighted from the planes with a stern, concentrated step. Long after they had already left the skies of the island behind them, the passengers' commotion continued unabated, and none of them turned to look at the vanishing mountain ranges or wondered about the destiny of the islanders in their blue-shuttered houses in the mountains.

What happened next Berenov found hard to explain to himself in his usual terms. His thoughts swelled unnaturally, like bladders, and were slowly dragged, sometimes toward his spine and sometimes in the direction of his legs, where they remained for a long time. His efforts to sharpen his eyes resulted in semi-opaque sight, as if his lids had already turned into whorls. But Berenov no longer needed these means of communication in order to abandon himself to the rustle flowing through his boughs. In all the branches the splashing of the sap grew louder, and the fleshy leaves burst from their skins and gave off a constant swishing of friction and whispers.

The green plastic armchair bent beneath the burden of the foliage which had already covered most of the room. The branches surprised the spiders out of their webs, some of them blocked the door, and the first of the dark leaves began pushing their way outside through the slits in the blinds.

Retrospectively, it was hard to estimate how much time had passed, the growth intensifying, until Berenov's door was torn down. He himself had already sailed beyond the realm of words. And even if possible, it is doubtful that he would have agreed to talk.

Fragmentary evidence alone survived the last fire—a few aerial photographs of the burning island, and stories full of contradictions by sailors somewhat the worse for drink, who at the time were on the deck of a ship crossing the island's horizon.

From these sources it appeared that a stir of preparation was felt in the mountain villages before the flames broke out. In the yards, baskets were filled with fruit and decorated with flowers. Embroidered white shirts, smelling faintly of sawdust, were taken out of the chests, and from the villages little, white-clad processions set out to climb to the mountain peaks. The flames, which had already begun to billow in the virgin forests at the heart of the island, pursued the climbers, and it sometimes seemed as if they were advancing in one united camp.

In the distance the island shores looked like gigantic embers cast into the waves. Intermittently the sea retreated from the fire and the sparks, and then it rushed back and swept boiling rocks and lumps of earth into its depths.

On the peaks circled by walls of fire, the island elders moved, nodding their heads and waving their hands, and behind them followed the young men, the women, and the children in a tight chain. The elders quickened the tempo, and behind them the youngsters' bodies pulsed rhythmically in a circle, in the flickering white of their embroidered clothes.

The burned pieces of land were rocked by the waves until the ashes were washed away. And when they sunk into the depths of the sea the fire, too, subsided.

The experts, quite rightly, raised their eyebrows and dismissed this unreliable evidence, together with the testimony of the sole surviving islander—an old man who had accidently remained behind on the mainland. He mumbled something about a city hidden in the ocean depths and about the gates of water and fire which would break open in years to come.

The scientific publications of that year omitted these details. But they definitely confirmed the fact of the disappearance of the island and its population—the last remnants of a society which had degenerated due to the debilitating influence of living continuously in the shade of forests.

When neighbors tore down Berenov's door, the room was full of a dense forest smell. This is not the place to dwell on the details of the manner in which he was evacuated. All that needs to be mentioned is the day, a particularly hot one, of the funeral itself which was attended, in spite of everything, by all those who honored the memory of Berenov, the clerk and loyal citizen from the third floor. To the embarrassment of the mourners, the gigantic coffin did not fit into the black van and was loaded onto its roof. When it was opened next to the grave, the green monster was once more revealed, and the mourners, overcome with nausea, stifled their retching in their handkerchiefs.

None of those present could possibly have guessed that

the shudder which passed through the foliage at that moment was not simply the stirring of the leaves in the breeze, but the convulsion of joy which seized hold of Berenov when his leaves merged at last with the fertile land, for whose warmth he had so greatly longed.

HOLD ON TO THE SUN

Some of the old neighborhoods of Jerusalem give me rather a strange feeling as I pass through them, as if they existed only for as long as I traverse them, springing up mysteriously from somewhere or other, my own imagination, perhaps, or even memories predating my birth, to stand there before I enter. Quickly the laundry is hung out on the long balconies, and children in black caftans come out to resume their games. The silence that always prevails after I pass has led me to the peculiar conclusion that behind my back, alley by alley, the neighborhood vanishes. This, too, is the reason for the habit which I have formed of never turning my head, and never looking back at these places.

For years I have refrained from expressing this feeling, even to myself, and when it sometimes awoke in me, even after I had emerged from these neighborhoods into other streets, I would reject it as firmly as a man dismissing the legends of some distant land and time. What finally led me to spend days on end examining it—without, however,

193

solving the riddle—was the following incident, which did not, apparently, happen by chance nor was it by chance that it happened where it did happen.

At the time I was busy working on my study of the history and sources of Jewish liturgy, comparing ancient versions of the daily evening prayer. I was vaguely aware of the existence of another old Prayer Book, which I had grounds to believe might contain, if not exactly a different version, at least a rare interpretation of the evening prayer and the time appointed for its recitation. The reference was hastily jotted down on an old index card, dating to a period before I undertook my study, which accounts for the slipshod nature of the notes. I may have copied them inaccurately from a manuscript, or taken them down during one of the lectures given by my late teacher who passed away many years ago.

According to my notes, this interpretation of the evening prayer refers to the light of the moon as it was before it was shrunk, and instructs believers to say the prayer with special rejoicing, "You should follow the sun in its sinking and the moon in its rising," and say with devout intent: "With wisdom Thou openeth the gates of the heavens, and with understanding Thou altereth the seasons." And when you say, "Thus hast Thou created day and night," you should concentrate intently on the words 'Day' and 'Night,' and attach all your joy to layla, Night, which is a resorting of the Hebrew letters of yahal—"He will illuminate"—and the extra letter "L." And you should attach your joy chiefly to that "L" of layla, which has the numerical value of thirty and stands for the darkness in the moon on the thirtieth day of the lunar month. The above is the secret of the impregnation of darkness by yahal, which is the light of the Seven Days of Creation, the Everlasting Light.

And the interpretation states furthermore that a believer should perform this deed in great secrecy, so that nothing at all of it be divulged. And he should exert himself greatly in its performance, so that he gain the upper hand over others who conspire falsely and delay the opening of the gates of Heaven. Such ones give rise to dissension between the sun and the moon and seek in their sin to stop the seasons in their appointed rounds and to bring, God forbid, a different light into the world.

And at the end of these notes I found, to my great astonishment, the following: There are some who say that a believer should start right now combining the morning, afternoon, and evening prayers. As if the words of the Prophet had already come to be, "The sun shall be no more thy light by day, neither for brightness shall the moon give light unto thee: But the Lord shall be unto thee an everlasting light." And I do not know whether these words actually figured in the old Prayer Book or were no more than a supposition on the part of my late teacher, or perhaps even my own part in those distant days.

For a long time I postponed going into the matter, but as I approached the conclusion of my study I realized that I would betray the truth if I failed to track down that Prayer Book and quote the relevant passages. My search in the National Library came to naught. Neither there, nor among the microfilmed manuscripts did I find any trace of it. Nor did I succeed in eliciting from the few friends of my university days any further details regarding my teacher's lectures on the subject of "Interpretations of the Evening Prayer." In the end, I came to believe that I had not only made a mistake in copying down the title of the Prayer Book, its date of publication, and the place where it was printed, but that the whole business was no more than barren speculation which I had once entertained . . .

Nevertheless, one day after completing my daily quota of writing, I set out to search for the missing Prayer Book in the book shops of the city's old neighborhoods. I went from shop to shop and to my repeated questions the booksellers replied—whether out of laziness, resentment, or because they were too busy to be bothered—that they did not know if they had it in their stock. They went on to recommend, however, that I look for myself since it was always possible that an old, forgotten volume might turn up somewhere in the shop. In this way I searched through many a dark backroom, where books in black bindings climbed to the ceiling, without finding what I was looking for.

I walked on, down narrow alleys and under stone archways, distracted both by the vertigo which always grips me when I spend hours reading the titles of rows of books upside down—climbing up and down the ladders does not improve matters—and by my suspicion that all my efforts were in vain. In the meantime it grew late, and as always in these old neighborhoods, I was filled with anxiety lest I should not be able to find my way out. As I was trying to decide whether to continue my search or whether it might not be wiser to stop now and attempt to retrace my steps, I saw, near the place where I was standing, a gap between two houses leading to a narrow passage. A shaft of light from the sinking sun penetrated the entrance, and but for the fact that it was thus illuminated, I have little doubt I would not even have noticed it, let alone entered.

To my surprise the passage led to a rather long quadrangle, lined on both sides by one or two storied buildings, all of whose entrances, both upstairs and down, housed little shops and market stalls. Because of the large space opening up between the houses, a broad, white band of sky was suddenly revealed. At its edge, above the tin roofs of the balconies, the moon was already hanging, waiting lightless like a pale assassin for its appointed time.

I had almost given up hope of finding the Prayer Book. And it was only a sense of duty which impelled me to go into the shops selling secondhand articles and ritual artifacts to inquire if by any chance such and such a Prayer Book, printed at such and such a date, in such and such a place, had not remained in their stock from times gone by. Finally, however I reached a cul-de-sac, with a synagogue wall on one side and various dilapidated objects, stools, cupboards, and sky-blue painted prayer stands on the other. At its bottom stood a little shop selling secondhand books, old brochures, and postcards with engravings of landscapes.

I could not see the bookseller and assumed that he must be busy arranging shelves in the inner rooms, which to judge by the confusion reigning in the front of the shop must have been totally chaotic. While I waited for him, I was happy to discover, after my wearisome search, the shop's engraved postcards and illustrated brochures. I leafed absentmindedly through some of them which I took from a shelf in one of the corners.

(When I think now, it is clear to me that I stood in precisely that corner only because the faint light entering from the cul-de-sac fell there, while the rest of the shop, apart from this narrow rectangle of light, was already in semi-darkness.)

I must confess that at first the album in question did not attract my attention. I was in the middle of perusing an illustrated pamphlet about road construction in the Ottoman Empire, when the gleaming spine of one of the books caught my eye. When I took it down, I saw that its cover, which must have been magnificent in its time, was made of red paper, and it was apparently the glistening of this red color which had attracted me.

It was an album of exquisitely beautiful photographs of landscapes at sunset. Although the old photographs had already faded, an almost dazzling light still emanated from them. It was obviously an artist's eye which had perceived and immortalized these sights. There was no word of explanation accompanying the pictures, yet at the same time it seemed to me, as I paged through them, that these many and varied sunsets were connected by some deliberate intention which would surely be revealed at the end.

The photographs at the end of the book showed, over and over again, with a particular kind of insistence, the same mountain looming out of a dense tangle of southern vegetation, like an oblong fruit, or the protruding breast of an island maiden, with the sea stretching flat and solid behind it. But it was only after looking at a number of pictures of this oblong mountain that I realized what it was that had aroused my astonishment: although all the surrounding landscape was covered by a luxuriant growth of palms, banana plants, and gigantic ferns of a species unfamiliar to me, the mountain itself was unnaturally bald, so that the light streaming from the low sun onto its slopes seemed brighter than ever.

The last photograph showed the same mountain again, with no change whatsoever. The album was finished, and I was left with the feeling that I still did not possess the key which was to have been revealed at the end. I went on paging disappointedly through the index of sites where the photographs had been taken, and as I glanced through it, a number of pages which had been stuck into the index (and which apparently had been printed separately, since neither the paper nor the print resembled those of the rest of the album), slipped into my hands. As soon as I saw the title on top of the first page: "From the estate of P., Artist-Photographer," I began eagerly reading in the fading daylight which still illuminated the corner where I was standing what follows here:

"I was engaged upon the final preparation for publishing the album. I had already sent the material to the printers to make the impressions, and all that now remained was the last photograph, upon whose completion everything— yes, everything—depended. I was about to embark upon my seventh and last voyage to the island of G. in South Asia, and this time I was confident that I would be able to take the picture.

"In the meantime my affairs brought me to the little town of M. in the Midwest, where I was invited to a garden party on the lake. I was excited at the thought of my approaching journey, and since I knew none of the other guests, and my host was preoccupied by his duties, I seated myself on the lawn facing the lake and abandoned myself to my reflections. As I gazed at the white sailing boats, I busied myself with making a mental list of the things I'd still have to take care of when I stopped over in the city to pick up the filter I'd specially built for the last photograph.

"While I was enjoying the respite from the noisy party, someone suddenly bumped into me. It was a young man of about thirty in a state of such extreme agitation that he lost his balance and almost spilled the contents of the plate on me. I expected him to apologize and continue on his way, instead of which, to my astonishment, he addressed me by my name which he kept repeating incredulously, even after I'd more than once affirmed that I was indeed he, and that my peculiar profession was, indeed, that of photographer. Without so much as a by your leave, the young man sat down next to me, seized hold of my hand as if to prevent me from getting up, and speaking rapidly, with hardly a pause for breath, embarked upon the following story:

'At that time, I was busy completing my studies on the West Coast, and all my hopes were pinned on the future. My wife, A., encouraged me during those long nights of burning the midnight oil and gladdened my heart with the happy details she kept adding to our castles in the air. One day we were strolling through the old quarter of the city, when we chanced upon a shop selling books and *objets d'art*, where a selection of your photographs of sunsets was exhibited.'

(When I heard this, my annoyance at the young intruder instantly melted away, and the old fears suddenly seized hold of me, the fears which had haunted me ever since I'd been tempted by my publisher to agree to holding an exhibition, even before the last picture was ready. However, I skillfully disguised this violent reaction, and the young man, who'd noticed nothing, continued his story with the same agitation as before and without letting go of my hand.)

'A. and I had always loved the sunset, even more ardently since becoming acquainted with its hues in that city on the coast. But your photographs enchanted us anew, and when we discovered among them a picture of our favorite view, from the hills opposite the shore, we decided in our enthusiasm that I would take more time off from my studies and that leaving the exhibition, we would set out immediately for the hills. The sunset that evening was hazy, with the sun descending through a vaporous sky. But thanks to your picture, the view held us spellbound. A. was particularly affected by the sight, and she declared, with a firmness uncharacteristic of her that we would have to come back to see the sunset there on the longest day of the year.

'Since I was completely absorbed during those spring months in preparing my final exams, I paid no attention to the changes in the weather and failed to see to it that A. was properly dressed when she left the house. For ever since that day she'd been overcome by restlessness, and she'd spend hours on end walking, in order to quiet herself and refrain from disturbing me. And thus, when she was out walking one afternoon, she caught a chill and fell ill.

'I divided my days between my books and the preparation of her medicines and shared in the astonishment of the doctors at the strange stubbornness with which the illness took hold of her. In the middle of June she was still bedridden, but this didn't stop her from reminding me of our decision to go out to the hills at sunset on the longest day of the year. When her fever rose, she'd become delirious and say strange things about *holding on to the sun*, which at the time I thought was a hallucination. When the longest day came, none of my pleas or the doctors' orders availed, and she insisted on going out to the hills facing the ocean.

'When we set out, she was more excited than I'd ever seen her, with the flush on her cheeks conspicuous against the pallor of her face. We stood on the hills and watched the great ball of light sinking slowly toward the horizon. I didn't notice anything out of the ordinary which might distinguish this sunset from the sunset on any other evening, although, as always, I marveled at the shades of purple, red, and yellow which suffused the sea and the sky. But A. was beside herself, and didn't take her eyes off the sun suspended in the sky. So frail was she after her prolonged illness, that the early summer wind pierced her like a freezing gale, and her whole body trembled. She held my hand with all her might. I can still feel the terrible force with which her slender fingers gripped me!

'At first she was ecstatic, but from the moment the sun touched the water line, her face fell. And with the same speed of the sun disappearing behind the horizon, A. darkened right before my eyes, and her fingers weakened their grip on my hand.

'I got her home as quickly as I could, and when I put

her to bed she kept repeating, "We came too late." Once she even mentioned your name, angrily, and said that you'd understand. I called the doctors as soon as we got home, but by the time they arrived it was already over.

'Ever since A.'s death, I've gone back to that hill on the longest day of every year, and I always stand there in the same confusion. I also went back to the old quarter, but I couldn't find your photographs, and to tell the truth, I was no longer able to locate the shop where we first saw them. From the few people who were able to tell me something about you, I learnt that you'd gone to South Asia on a photography expedition, and hadn't been back to our part of the world for several years. Nevertheless, my pain at the death of A. had always been connected with a sense of obligation to tell you about the circumstances of her dying. I felt that until I did so I would not have fulfilled her wish, even though she never expressed it explicitly.'

"The young man was so moved by his tale that he didn't notice what I was going through, and by the time he looked at me, I'd already succeeded in controlling my emotions and in concealing them from him. I contended that I didn't understand what he was talking about, and said I was sorry with all my heart (which was quite true) for the death of A., his wife, although I hadn't had the honor of making her acquaintance. A silence fell, and both of us looked at the lake, where the sun was then sinking behind the ribbon of mist encircling the horizon and the spots of light on the boats' sails were suddenly blotted out. After a prolonged moment of oppressive silence, the young man stood up and was swallowed up among the guests.

"I suffered pangs of conscience for the way I'd treated the young man, but I had had no choice. Even now, who knows what dire consequences might yet ensue from the old, newly awakened fears; who knows if it will still be possible to amend what his story has wrought.

"As I write these lines, our ship has already sailed past the coasts of Ceylon and Java, and in three days time it will let me off at the only port on the island of G . . . The album is already at the printers, all that is missing is the last photograph, in order . . . (and perhaps I'd better not write anything explicit down yet). On my previous six trips I've succeeded in establishing close ties with the people of the K. tribe, and this time I—the first foreigner—will take part in their endeavor. Yes, ever since I discovered their project on my first trip, a change has taken place in my whole attitude toward what I had up to then been doing unconsciously— thinking that it was only the beauty of the scenery which compelled me to photograph the sunset. Ever since then, I've been waiting with them, and preparing myself with the means at my disposal for the appointed day.

"Time and time again I've conjured up the ceremony from the stories I've heard, and each time I'm filled with new admiration for the people of the tribe of K. and their ancient belief. How they learned to determine with their miraculous methods of measuring the longest day of the year, despite the minimal time changes in their region. How once in a generation—only thus could they persist in their efforts without being utterly annihilated—all the members of the tribe, from the age of puberty on, go up to the mountain before dawn. Oh, how well I know that ascending path, the view it affords of the South Sea, the wind which blows on its peak. How well I know the jealousy with which the tribe has guarded those slopes all these years, lest any alien stalk take root upon them and prevent the sun from holding on to the mountain.

"They say the excitement of the members of the tribe on that day is so great that the drumming and singing continue without a break from dawn. And my own humble experience can testify that the very thought of the light not stopping, the spark of a belief in the sun not setting, is enough for boundless joy to explode. All morning long the tribesmen devote themselves to impregnating the women with the souls of light, and at noon the women walk about in the warm breeze with bodies satiated as suns, while the men follow them drunk with hope, as if this longest day were already the beginning of an endless dawn.

"When the afternoon arrives, the people of the tribe stand on the top of the mountain, which shines like a round belly, and follow the movement of the sun as it begins to go down to the sea. When the sun stands still, not far from the horizon at the edge of the ocean, they lift up their arms toward it and hold it with all their might. They pull it like a lever toward its reflection on the mountain, and add all their power to its own efforts to rise, full and strong, to the zenith of the sky, from where it will never move again.

"Their efforts then are so awesome, that when the sun slips from their grasp and sinks beneath the sea, they collapse like flies, too weak to hang onto the slippery slopes in order to break their downward slide. And thus, immediately after sunset on the longest day of the year, once in every generation, the people of the tribe are dashed to pieces against the dense vegetation at the bottom of the mountain.

"There is no need to dwell here on the way in which I've been waiting with them, for the past seven years, for the month of June in the year 192 . . . Six times I've returned to the mountain on that particular day. I've checked whatever lies within my power to check. And all, I may say, is now ready.

"There are two days to go before we anchor at the island of G., and another five before the next effort. In the meantime I spend my days on the deck, watching the Asian sailors who speak in their own tongues and leave me alone with my thoughts. And in the evening I wage lengthy campaigns of card games against the Dutch captain. Yet I cannot silence the old fears. What the young man told me about the death of his wife, A., in the city on the coast, confirmed in a most terrible way my apprehensions about the premature exhibition of my photographs. Who knows if A. was the only one affected. And who can tell what threat now hangs over the K. tribe, once their endeavors were made public. Ah, my photographer's hubris, my insolent insistence on fixing with an iron eye that which seeks to sink in secrecy . . .

"Two days are left in which to live in hope, two more days until I share the prayers of the admired people of the K. tribe . . . "

I returned the interrupted text to its place between the pages of the index, and began leafing once more in great agitation through the photographs, in all of which the disk of the setting sun shone through the dimness of age. I began, my heart pounding, turning the pages rapidly in order to get another look at that mountain rising in its fullness to face the sea, when I thought I heard the sound of footsteps in the inner room. Only then did I become conscious of the darkening shop, which I had completely forgotten as I heatedly devoured the photographer's words. And I quickly put the album down on the wooden stand. Its cover glowed in the sparse light and was reflected like a dull shadow of rubies on the wooden boxes containing the engraved post-cards. Once more I was drawn to its radiance and I was just about to stretch out my hand to pick it up again, when the book seller appeared in the dark doorway, thin and bearded, with his black hat almost covering his face. Hardly aware of what I was doing, I tried to hide the album but the man stopped me with a gesture of his hand, and asked me what I wanted.

I almost replied—to hold on to the sun, but controlled myself immediately and asked for the old Prayer Book.

"What do you need that book for?" the bookseller asked angrily.

I mumbled something about the research I had been conducting for years, but he cut me short and announced firmly, "You have no need of that book!"

"You're right, sir," I agreed in order to appease him, and with my heart beating, I inquired, "Is the gentleman himself familiar with the Prayer Book in question?"

Never before had I yearned so hungrily to read that marvelous interpretation of the evening prayer, never before had I believed so fervently in the possibility of penetrating its secret intentions, of grasping the meaning of the Everlasting Light. And from a vast distance, from beneath layers which seemed to me to have been deadened a long time ago, at that moment I felt a fierce excitement, perhaps hope awakening in me and piercing me like a burning ember. Me, the scholar of liturgical sources, who knew nothing all these years but notes and old manuscripts.

Making no attempt to conceal his hostility, the bookseller repeated, "You have no need of that book!"

"But are you familiar with it, sir, do you have it in your shop?"

"You have nothing to look for here!" he almost shouted. "We've been closed for hours."

With one step he crossed the dark, paper-filled room and slammed the iron grill down over the door through which I'd entered. Then he returned, removed the album from the wooden stand, pushed it back hastily onto its place on the shelf, and pointed to the door to the inner room, "Through here, through here," he said, hitting me roughly on the back to hurry me up, and disappearing through the dark doorway.

In the inner room, too, the stacks of books reached to the ceiling, and here, too, old brochures were scattered over high wooden stands.

"Through here, through here," the bookseller scoldingly indicated the back door, and this time, too, he hurried through it before me.

In this way we passed through a number of inner rooms without stopping in any of them, all of whose walls were covered with rows and rows of black books, tightly crammed together. Finally we crossed a little paved courtyard at the far end of which the bookseller impatiently opened an iron gate.

Before I had time to ask the bookseller where we were and how to find my way out of the neighborhood, I heard the gate barred behind me. The long square on whose edge I was standing was already almost completely dark, and the full moon commanded it like a petrified monarch. In the middle of the square a lamp suspended from a high wooden post cast a small circle of light around it. As I stood there wondering which direction to take, a few children in black caftans ran past me tugging a black cloth canopy, which flapped in heavy folds behind their heads. They rushed toward the lamp without noticing me as they ran.

I began walking, without turning my head to look back at the gate from which I had emerged. A man in a broad-brimmed hat passed me, his head bowed. I hurried after him to the far end of the square, where he disappeared into the depths of a dark alley. For some time I strayed through unfamiliar passageways and empty courtyards, until suddenly, without any change in the silence shrouding the houses, I found myself outside the neighborhood. A bus standing in the road started its engine. I hurried to climb on before it moved off, and was carried away by its swaying motion.

Once, and only once, I returned to that old neighborhood and tried to retrace the steps which had led me to the shop selling old books and engraved postcards. Despite all my efforts, I could not find the narrow, paved passage leading to the marketstalls, nor the stairs of the alley which led to the quadrangle. For hours I wandered through the alleys, but all in vain. A number of times I imagined that I was nearing my destination, only to realize my mistake. But at the bottom of my heart I was not in the least surprised at my failure to find what I was looking for. For I had always been prone to the peculiar sensation that these old neighborhoods were nothing but figments of my imagination, memories which materialized only when I passed through them and then vanished behind my back.

In the deep night, darkness descended fully. And when I stood outside the neighborhood, I groped my way past the black hills of a region where I had never been before. I did not even know the number of the bus that took me through the labyrinth of crooked roads back to the street where I live.

In the days that followed, days which I spent at the printers correcting and recorrecting the proofs of my study, I felt like a guilty man whose days were numbered. I concluded the final preparations for the publication of my book with a heavy heart, and without saying a word to anyone about what was distressing my soul. Even in the book's preface, I did not mention the name of the old Prayer Book, nor the existence of another, different interpretation of the meaning of the evening prayer.

Many years have passed since then. My book came out long ago and its pages are bound and gray. The living memory has grown increasingly dimmer, and with it that unexpected hope, like a passionate dream, which I have never dared to call by its name. Only this tale is left to me. Buried among my notes.

FACING EVIL: THOUGHTS ON A
VISIT TO AUSCHWITZ
(ESSAY, 2006)

Discussions are currently underway about restoring the Auschwitz Museum, which was established on the grounds of the concentration camp two years after World War II. I visited the museum last summer as part of a writing journey in which I followed in the footsteps of my mother. When I returned to Israel after the visit, bewildered by what I had seen, I was asked to share my thoughts with the Auchwitz museum's advisory committee.

My first visit to Auschwitz was thirty years ago, alone, as a young Israeli doctoral student living abroad in Paris. That was before I began to cope with the past of my mother, Rina Govrin, who went on the death march from Auschwitz to Bergen-Belsen; and it was before I began to come to terms with the short life of her son, my half-brother Marek Laub, who was sent to the gas chambers at the age of eight after his father was murdered. That was back when Communist Poland was largely closed off to the Western world. In the empty, abandoned spaces of Auschwitz-Birkenau, I found only a small group of Polish schoolchildren in the late autumn chill, as if time had stopped. And there, in the heart of the menacing silence of the biggest cemetery in the world, echoed the rage to shout that which lies outside the human capacity for language and imagination.

Dazed, I walked among the blocs of Auschwitz and across the grounds of Birkenau. And there, facing the silence of the place, I understood that I couldn't go on denying the past, though it had seemed so easy in the Tel Aviv of my childhood, or in the Paris of the 1970s. From then on, much of what I wrote was, in some way, an echo of my mother's story.

Last summer, I returned as part of a "delegation of two" with Rachel-Shlomit, my older daughter, who had lost her grandmother when she was a baby. It was a full twenty years after my mother's death, but I traveled with the voices of the women who had survived alongside her and who had conveyed to me, one by one, several strands of the story she had silenced. On that summer morning, the museum was teeming with masses of visitors from all over the world, both individuals and groups, only a few from Israel. This time, when we were swallowed up among those congregating at the museum exhibits, what was most apparent to me was the mighty process of erasing. Then and now.

Among the other tourists, who were divided into groups, we were led by a Polish guide on an official tour.

Following now in my own footsteps as well, I passed through the museum exhibits for the second time in my life. As the visit progressed, I was confronted by a sense of internal paralysis. I felt the renewed shock of facing the trap of destruction—the ramp where the transports arrived straight to death, and its alternative: forced labor, starvation, human experimentation laboratories, and only then to the gas chambers with cans of Zyklon B and the ovens. And the remains, heaps of remains: the shoes, the eyeglasses, the brushes, the hair. But at the same time, I was seized by another emptiness that grew stronger: the silence of millions of human beings who were murdered and tortured here. During the visit, they were once again swallowed up in the anonymity of mass numbers, in the facelessness of collective identity, in the deceptive glory of martyrdom. And they were swallowed, too, in the compressed piles of remains that stood as holy relics in glass display cases. Among the masses of visitors, their absence reverberated.

Auschwitz is a graveyard without a grave. The Nazi death factory murdered a million and a half people here, systematically wiping out their ashes and their memory. Those who were murdered have left no personal traces, and even in the museum, they practically do not exist—not as human beings. Not in their previous lives and not as they lived between the fences of the camp, in the blocs, the huts, the lines to death. The names of the dead or of the survivors aren't mentioned, and their photos are hard to find. Few have voices, and most of their stories remain untold. The museum doesn't show us the complexity of their responses, and they remain frozen for the most part as they appear in Nazi documentation. And so, facing the detailed exhibition of the face of evil, there is almost no echo in the Auschwitz Museum of the human experience in the camps. This is not at the center of the exhibition, nor are the many ways in which human beings stood tall or collapsed in the face of evil.

Feeling dizzy, I retreated from the groups of visitors. Despite myself, I felt like a collaborator. As if with a one-way gaze, the visitor to Auschwitz continues to wipe out the humanity of the inmates, reducing them to a pile of organic matter that will decay over the years. And so it wasn't just the heaps of hair that dismayed me, but also their graying color (even though, according to the museum's documents, the hair underwent preservation in the museum labs in 1968, when a hundred kilos of dust were removed from it, and its "natural color" was restored).

When confronted with the itinerary of our tour through the torture blocs and the paths that led to death, I felt like I was waiting in line with the crowds that had thronged, all throughout history, to take part in the macabre tradition of the spectacle of death—from the medieval scenes of hell to the curio tours of the torture chambers, up to the thrill of the haunted house ride in amusement parks. The deep fascination with the culture of horror shows still lives on even after Auschwitz, after Rwanda and Darfur, and also after September 11 (which won Stockhausen's praise for its "aesthetic force").

I sat helplessly at the side of the path between the blocs, and I knew that, as with the tradition of the macabre, so on the visit to Auschwitz, the good ones would come out better and the bad ones worse. When confronted with evil, some will whisper a vow of justice and others will repeat the wicked catechisms of the grand executioners.

Can it be that, despite its noble intentions, the Auschwitz Museum is essentially a memorial to the Genius of Evil? Will it contribute to the unbearable dizzying swirl of terms such as holiness, victimhood, martyrdom? Will it enhance the vertigo which, perhaps, began with the victimizing sacred concept of "Holo-Caust" (burnt offering; burnt whole), coined by François Mauriac in his introduction to Eli Wiesel's *Night*, and which has since become the "desired term" in the global "contest" of blood for the status of victim, and for the venal sanctification of martyrdom and death (including that of suicide bombers)?

But Auschwitz was not established by God or created by Satan. Man built Auschwitz, and man tortured human beings to death in it. The victims of Auschwitz didn't die for the "Sanctification of the Name," but struggled for the "Sanctification of life," as Rabbi Isaac Nussbaum declared during his last months in the Warsaw Ghetto. In the camps, man was revealed, in his depths and his heights.

Yet, how to make the human voice heard in the pit of hell? How to memorialize the ways they stood facing evil? How to listen to the many facets of meaning revealed in the heart of evil? How to recall the despair, the weakness, the strength, the cruelty, the brotherhood, the compassion, the heresy and the belief in God, in man? How to learn the extreme lesson of the camp, of what Victor Frankel termed "man's search for meaning"?

On that afternoon at Auschwitz, I didn't return to the groups of visitors. Through the exhibitions, the blocs, and the huts, I tried to hold on to my mother's story—the story that she, refusing to be a victim, was determined to erase when she came to Israel in 1948. And so she underwent an operation to remove the number from her arm, and her story was silenced until she died. I held on to the threads of that story that had been hidden in my childhood and that I had pieced together in recent years from relatives and from the nine women, the *zenerschaft*, as they were called in the camps, with whom my mother had survived Plaszow, Birkenau, Auschwitz, the death march and Bergen-Belsen. How, after their families were murdered, they strengthened one another amidst the torture, the forced labor, the hunger; and how they helped one another, lit Hanukkah candles in bloc 24, shared their bread, tried to go on laughing, to go on maintaining a human image. I pictured my uncle, Tovek Poser, who threw himself onto the electrified fence of Auschwitz, and eight-year-old Marek who was sent to death with the children's transport from Plaszow.

My legs buckling, next to my daughter, I came to the birches behind the chimneys of the crematoria. In the distance, the voice of an Israeli teacher could be heard reading excerpts of personal testimonies to her students. Without a word, I searched for a moment for a sign carved in a tree. My mother's friend had told me that as they were waiting at the entrance to the gas chambers, when some were saying their final confessions, my mother had walked among the birches. She was seeking a sign that Marek might have left for her. I looked for a sign, too. A personal one. When I found none, I marked on one of the trunks the letter M—the first letter of our names: Marek. Michal. And then, in this place steeped in smoke and ashes, I said kaddish.

When the Russian army entered the gates of Auschwitz in January 1945, the camp was almost completely empty. Most of the prisoners had been sent on a death march to labor and extermination camps throughout Poland and Germany. What remained in Auschwitz were the silent remnants of the machinery of annihilation, and the Nazi lists, photos, and other forms of documentation. Those were the artifacts that comprised most of the original exhibition.

The Auschwitz Museum was established in 1947 by the Polish government. A group of Polish survivors fought to preserve the remnants so as to thwart the Nazis' attempt at complete obliteration, and to collect evidence of the crimes that were committed at Auschwitz. Later on, it was decided to make no changes in the site—to respect it as a graveyard, and to preserve it as it was at the time of the Liberation. The piles of personal items, the hair, the blocs, the huts, the remains of the crematoria became silent witnesses, and Auschwitz-Birkenau Camp became a place of memory. A place of testimony and condemnation. But, presenting the machinery of death and torture is only half the story. The other half is the story of human beings facing evil.

The stories of the inmates were revealed very gradually. Only years later were diaries of the members of the *sonderkommando** dug up out of the piles of ashes in the chimneys of the crematoria and added to the exhibition. The voices of the survivors were late in being heard too, either because of all those who were unwilling to listen, or because the survivors were trying to put the past aside and establish a new life for themselves. "Your mother didn't

* (German) Work unit consisting of Nazi death camp prisoners forced to assist the mass killing process during the Holocaust.

have to talk about Auschwitz, she *was* there," one of her survivor freinds told me recently.

In the first years, society could bear to listen only to the bold voices of the underground fighters and the rebels. They resonated clearly in a world that had fought the Nazis, and in a nascent State of Israel in the midst of its own war for existence. It was years until the concept of heroism could also echo in a piece of bread given by one prisoner to another, in a prayer of the "Days of Awe" handwritten by memory in the absence of prayer books, in the ability to love in the camp, in the gallows humor, or in the voice of Primo Levi, who recited Dante on his way to pick up a pot of soup. Years passed until the stigma of "like sheep to the slaughter" began to fade—we had to first endure the murder of the Israeli athletes at the Munich Olympics to prove that hostages, even able-bodied ones, may actually be helpless vis-à-vis their captors. Years passed until the rage of survival gained recognition and appreciation—the hasty marriages, the astonishing number of babies born in the DP camps, and the survivors' obstinate will to live. Years passed until the guilt of the survivors vis-à-vis the killed, and even more the guilt of society vis-à-vis the survivors, gave way to listening and documentation. At the last moment.

For sixty years, material has been collected in archives, libraries, and courts. We have testimonies, video interviews, conversations with children and grandchildren. Slowly the names of the dead were gathered, and the solitary voices coalesced into a great chorus of personal stories disassembling the anonymous mass of people-turned-numbers and restoring the faces to the millions who filled Auschwitz. Writing the mighty story of the human face.

The founders of the museum stopped the systematic suppression of all traces of Nazi atrocity. But the exhibits didn't stop the impulse of denial—as is demonstrated by the speeches of Iranian president Ahmadinejad culminating in the recent Holocaust Denial Conference in Tehran, or the many websites devoted to this cause which play saccharine music as they present Auschwitz as "a model work camp" with a "sauna" and an "orchestra" and a "hospital" . . .

Among the group of stone buildings and the expanses of crumbling huts, the story of humanity is buried. Here, everyone comes to confront their own past: the children and grandchildren of the murderers and the murdered, of the torturers and the tortured, of those who stood on the side and those who reached out a hand. It is the meeting place of the human spirit. The meeting place and the place for the accounting of the soul. Here the battle for memory and meaning is waged, a battle that is ongoing and urgent— a battle that will determine the face of our world.

Auschwitz wasn't on another planet; it was an extreme manifestation of the human soul. This is the place to hear the voices of man. To listen to the trenchant lesson of the camps: the lesson of how man can create a machinery of annihilation, and the lesson about the ways to hold on to life and to meaning—the founding lesson of humanity. This is the place where the visitor comes to listen to the voices of man, and from here she will carry them to her home to turn to them in the crucial moments of her life. Inevitably, we will all have our own moments of accounting—in situations when we ourselves will be strong or will be held hostage, when we will be asked to choose between turning our backs or holding out our hands.

In a new techno-savvy Auschwitz Museum, visitors should have access to an enormous human mosaic of voices and stories. Voices of the murdered and voices of the survivors, voices of the second and third generation, and of artists, thinkers, and psychologists. A mighty chorus of voices that will resound through the silence of the graveyard. And the visitor will lend an ear to the voices he will choose, the voices he will encounter, the voices with whom he will converse in his soul.

In the bus that took my daughter and me and the other visitors out of Auschwitz, there was silence. I looked at the numb, withdrawn people. There were Europeans and Americans, Asians and Africans, and a young hippie couple with Tartar features who were resting, their heads leaning on one another. The setting sun gilded the summer fields and the faces of the passengers, and bathed the gentle motion of the bus in a soft light.

In Auschwitz, a universal story of humanity was written. A story with many voices, many moments of people facing Evil. A living memory, like the Exodus from slavery in Egypt, compelling, demanding, of every single human to view themselves as if they, too, had come out of Auschwitz.

SELICHOT * IN KRAKOW:
MIGRATIONS OF A MELODY
(ESSAY, 2007)

The only one of my mother's melodies to remain is the sing-song of the *shamosh*† from the Remuh Synagogue in Krakow, as he passed at night through the streets of the ancient ghetto, Kazimierz, knocking on the window shutters and waking the Jews for *selichot*, the early morning service before the high holidays. "*Yidelekh, yidelekh, tayere koshere yidelekh, shteyen oyf, shteyen oyf lavoydes haboyre uleslikhes.*" Jews, Jews, dear, kosher Jews, please rise, please rise to worship the Creator and for *selichot*.

My mother, Rina Poser-Laub Govrin left her beloved native city on the eighteenth of October, 1944, on a train going from the Plaszow labor camp to Auschwitz. By then, both her husband and son had been murdered. My mother never set foot in Krakow again.

Recently I was invited by the Polish Institute to participate in a cultural exchange program. I agreed only after

---

* (Hebrew) Jewish penitential poems and prayers leading up to Rosh Hashanah and Yom Kippur
† (Yiddish) assistant synagogue manager

receiving assurance that, alongside the official visit, I would be able to join in the annual march commemorating the expulsion of Krakow's Jews. In 1942 the Jews were banished from their homes to a ghetto in the Podgorze district, and in 1943, after a series of murderous *Aktionen*, those remaining were deported by foot to the Plaszow labor camp, whose construction, inspired by the sadism of its commander, Amon Göth, was undertaken on the grounds of the Jewish cemetery.

The Memorial March from the Podgorze district to Plaszow was set to take place on a Sunday morning. I therefore arrived on a train from Warsaw to Krakow on Friday afternoon, before sabbath. On the platform I was met by Sylvia, my official escort, a petite, shapely woman wearing a checkered coat—a perfect Polish beauty. I took down my suitcases and shamefacedly apologized for their weight. I found it hard to explain the anxiety that gripped me in anticipation of retracing the footsteps of my mother, of my murdered eight-year-old brother. And so, tormented by the migration of souls that I had embarked upon, I dragged with me on my journey all the books I deemed absolutely essential for my survival: Kafka, and Rilke, and Gebirtig, and Primo Levi, and Szymborska, and Bruno Schulz, and Viktor Frankl, and a *siddur*,* and a *mikraot gedolot*,† and *Noam*

---

* (Hebrew) A prayer book.
† (Hebrew) Often called a "Rabbinical Bible" in English, an edition that generally includes three distinct elements: the biblical text, the Aramaic translation, and biblical commentaries.

Elimelech by the Rebbe of Lizhensk,* weighing in all some sixty pounds . . .

Sylvia, delicate as she was, kept up a smile, even when, in her tiny car stuffed with baggage, we reached the small hotel with no elevator in Kazimierz, the ancient ghetto, and even as we athletically dragged the huge suitcase up floor after floor after floor. I was the one who broke down when I saw the cramped, dark attic I'd been allotted, with a skylight that barely illuminated the room's old wallpaper. I knew that if I spent three days there, including the march of returning souls, they'd have to carry me out straight to the loony bin. Sylvia, feeling responsible, was drenched in sweat. Sabbath drew near, and it was only by sheer luck that, at that last moment, a comfortable room was vacated in a hotel a few alleys away.

And so we set out, Sylvia with the small bags, and I with the suitcase full of selected classics of world literature, bumping along the paving stones of the ancient streets. But then, in the midst of a struggle to negotiate a turn in the road, the suitcase handle snapped. The suitcase stopped and the detached handle remained in my hand.

"What will we do!?" Sylvia was in a panic from the daze of Jewish wandering she had been thrust into. "It's ok," I said, trying to calm her. "I'll carry the suitcase like this." And immediately I began dragging the great weight God knows

* A classic Hasidic work by one of the founding Rebbes of the Hasidic movement.

how. But Sylvia's worry did not subside, sweat dripped from her brow, and her entire slender figure exuded despair. I knew I had to encourage her, and in a flash it came to me. "This reminds me of a song in Yiddish!" I called out, "Me without you, and you without me is like a handle without a door." With my breath short from the effort of dragging the suitcase, I began to sing the love song set in a waltz tempo, "*Ikh on dir un du on mir iz vi a kliamke on a tir* . . ."

And so, down the narrow streets of Estery and Jozefa, with one hand waving the broken handle and the other grasping the orphaned metal rod, I lugged the huge weight as if effortlessly and sang, "*Ikh on dir un du on mir iz vi a kliamke on a tir* . . . *ketzele, faygele, mayn*." The word "*kliamke*," handle, had found its way into Yiddish from Polish. The familiar word and the sweetness of the waltz calmed Sylvia down a bit, so that finally even she began to hum along with the irresistibly beautiful tune.

That evening, after prayers at the ancient Remuh Synagogue, I was invited to a sabbath meal held in the hall at the top of the half-deserted Hochschule Synagogue and organized by the young rabbi, Boaz Pash, who had been sent to Krakow from Israel. The modest meal, served at tables covered with paper tablecloths, drew a unique admixture of guests: two or three elderly members of the community, living in solitude and speaking tatters of Yiddish, several wildly excited women, some of whom had recently discovered that beneath their Polish biography a Jewish girl had been kept in hiding for the past sixty years, and who were now frantically trying to bridge over a lifetime, a group of goyim from France and Poland meeting in Krakow for discussions of goodwill, and a few young people who, having also one day discovered that ancestral Jewish blood was flowing in their veins, founded a group called "*Cholent.*"* They were the ones serving the simple food to this curious congregation.

I was seated at the foot of the table, facing the French. The young rabbi addressed the members of the community with fatherly warmth, made the blessings, went over the songs the guests knew, and encouraged them to say a few words. And so, between the modest courses, a young American who somehow wound up in Krakow got to deliver a "sermon." For a moment it seemed as if he were nostalgically recalling his Bar Mitzvah party, but then the young man, whose literary ambitions were apparently influenced by Henry Miller, led his story from the synagogue *bimah*† straight to the toilet, and to his uncle, who sighed while he masturbated in the midst of the celebration in one of the stalls. The lecherous grin was still on the young man's face when the door of the hall burst open, and in sallied two *shtreimels*‡ three feet high, and beneath them,

---

* (Yiddish) Special stew for Sabbath.
† (Hebrew) Pulpit.
‡ (Yiddish) Fur hat worn by many married Haredi (ultra orthodox) Jewish men, particularly members of Hasidic groups, on Sabbath and during Jewish holidays.

two white-bearded Jews wearing traditional *kapotas*.* "The Rabbi of Galicia and his *shamosh*," the whisper spread among the castaways seated at the table. The rabbi, an American who receives his appointment (and salary) from New York, gave a short speech in a thundering voice, after which he burst out in song in a yet more thundering voice, which seemed to emanate from an amplifier. At first the thickly bearded *shamosh* joined him, but when some of the emotional ladies also joined in the singing with their indecent feminine voices, the *shamosh* took off, and shortly after the rabbi departed as well, sternly carrying the weight of his enormous *shtreimel*.

The community of castaways was left fragmented and forlorn following the Sermon of the Toilet and the departure of the *shtreimels*. Confusion settled on the tables.

Suddenly the voice of the young rabbi rang out, "Michal, sing that song." What is he talking about, I thought, astonished. "What song?" "The one you sang in the street today." "What?! How do you know?" "I passed by and heard you singing. That's how I recognized you." The circumstances of my dizzying visit to Krakow rushed through my head, what had been told, what had been silenced, the pitiful state of the community, the rabbi's appeal, and I knew I had no choice but to do my part.

I sang the Yiddish love waltz. After the first time the

* (Yiddish) Long black coat worn by Haredi Jewish men.

guests at the tables hummed the tune. "Again!" called the rabbi, and the next time everyone sang, instinctively rocking from side to side and waving their hands, "*Ikh on dir un du on mir . . .* " By the third time, everyone rose to dance around the tables, with the young rabbi at the head, waving his arm.

The sudden echo of my private experience made me giddy. And then, when the dancing stopped, on impulse I declared, "I have another tune for you! From here, from Krakow." The excited ladies, the elders, the rabbi, all raised their faces to me when I began the sing-song of the *shamosh* from the Remuh Synagogue, which had reached my ears in my mother's voice, "*Yidelekh, yidelekh, tayere koshere yidelekh, shteyen oyf, shteyen oyf lavoydes haboyre uleslikhes.*" Jews, Jews, dear, kosher Jews, please rise, please rise to worship the Creator and for *selichot*.

The standing guests nodded their heads, listened; the flushed older women, the ardent youth, some of the Jewish elders hummed along in Yiddish, and the young Israeli rabbi repeated after me the tune that had been exiled from the streets of the ancient ghetto of Krakow and forgotten, "*Yidelekh, Yidelekh . . .* "

At a late hour we emerged, a small handful of guests summoned to Szeroka Square in the heart of Kazimierz. The large square was totally empty. "How does it go?" the rabbi asked, as he began chanting in the dark, "*Yidelekh . . .* " Following him, more voices joined in, "*Yidelekh, yidelekh, tayere koshere yidelekh, shteyen oyf, shteyen oyf lavoydes haboyre uleslikhes.*"

The façade of the Remuh Synagogue, and the great gate of the ancient cemetery, locked at that hour, shone white through the darkness. And in a melody's return, the singsong of the Remuh Synagogue *shamosh* echoed once more, across the destruction, and after so many years, passing as he once did through the nighttime streets, knocking on the shutters and waking the sleeping—the dead and the living—for *selichot*.

A CONVERSATION BETWEEN
MICHAL GOVRIN AND JUDITH G. MILLER
2009

On coming to writing . . .

JM: I'd like to start by situating the stories and the essays in this collection within your work as an Israeli writer. Here's my quick summary of your trajectory: You began writing poetry as a child in the 1960s and you still do. You direct theater; you have published two novels; you're writing a third; you've compiled the memoirs of your father and you're writing about your mother . . .

MG: And I have an unpublished first novel.

JM: Right! So where do your short stories fit within all this?

MG: The short stories arrived before the novels, and they were my first venture into prose writing. They emerged from the poetry, but from the beginning I felt a very great urge to tell a story—to catch the world in prose. So as I didn't yet feel like launching into a novel, the short stories imposed themselves, as much of my writing does.

JM: When was this?

MG: In the late 60s. That's when I started the first short story I ever wrote. It's not in this collection and I wrote it as though a movie script. It was a fantastic love story. And I think it shows something about the nature of my vision, even then. I see the world as visual narratives, and I think that also explains my need for theater, because in theater I can really see the characters. They appear on stage, as it were. My three modes: poetry, prose fiction, and theater all date from the same time, and they stem from the great influences and the great ambitions I've felt since adolescence.

JM: I know that coming back to this first collection of short stories has been an interesting voyage for you, because you wrote these stories in the 1970s and 1980s, and you hadn't really reread them until this summer when we started seriously revisiting the original translations into English from the Hebrew. How has this plunge back into the stories affected you?

MG: At first, I was very afraid of rereading them. Without your giving me a hand in this Dante-esque descent into what seemed like who knows what, I wouldn't have dared do it. I've been afraid that something from my old self would disturb me, that entering into the intimacy of the mind that created these stories would be a sacrilege, an attempt to deny time. But I must say that it's been a very powerful experience. I've come to recognize and appreciate that young person who wrote them and I give tribute to what that person was at that time, that person who's not me anymore. And then I also recognize my recurring themes, recurring needs, poetic needs—and I recognize the process. Suddenly to see life as a process, to see things that literally wrapped me up whole and that I took years to unravel . . . I now understand that what I theoretically believed about the power of adolescence is true.

JM: You mean that in adolescence one's deepest needs, one's desires are already in place?

MG: It's a moment of big potential in a life story, of powerful urges and desire, of a vivid encounter with the world of experience and of culture, and the time when the individual personality emerges from a person's heritage. Cracks and openings occur in your psyche and if you know how to respect and listen to them, they'll carry you all of your life. My departure from Israel, my going to Paris in the early 70s answered both an unconscious and a conscious need to direct my life in a way that would allow me to listen to these voices, to these urges. Otherwise, they may not have been granted the space they needed.

JM: This harks back to when we first met in Paris in 1972. Our work on these stories has also been a revelation to me, because in Paris we talked about ideas, we talked about theater; we went to the theater a lot together. We even did theater! But I was unaware of the kinds of things you were writing. You were very secretive about that.

MG: Because I didn't take my writing for granted. These short stories are also very moving for me because they represent my determination *to write*. I had a room to myself, a *chambre de bonne*—a very small room—I didn't know at that time about Virginia Woolf's notion. But the need to have a room for myself was strong. I also felt I had to camouflage it. Maybe out of insecurity, because who knows if you have the right to claim to be a writer in this world . . . Also, in terms of the subject matter, there was really the danger of exposing something scary about myself.

JM: So it was easier for you—and for me, I think—to be the good students we'd always been. To talk about our dissertations, our graduate studies, our theater work, while you had this secret writing life.

MG: Yes, but mind you my dissertation was on a parallel path to the short stories because it took me more and more into Jewish mysticism. That was my way of learning what I felt was needed for my writing career. I used my dissertation to get to what was most important in what I wanted to be in life, which was not a research person, but a writing person.

JM: Let's talk about the essays in this volume. In them you speak of going back to Poland, although it's not that you came from Poland but, rather, that's where part of your family's history is. In these journeys you discover your roots; you discover horrors, but also real communities, especially through art. How do we connect these essays to the stories?

MG: I'm very happy about these essays being included in this volume because they represent something I mentioned a minute ago—the fomenting of a theme, a life theme that evolves through time. They add a dynamic aspect to the collection. For example, the first essay, "Journey to Poland," was written in 1975, immediately upon returning from a journey that shattered something I had repressed. But I wrote the framing meditation around it in 1996 when my novel *The Name* was published in English. In the novel, I articulate through fiction this legacy of horror and community. "Facing Evil" and "Migrations of a Melody," which close the volume, date from 2006 and 2007 when I finally dared to start writing openly my mother's story. The essays document the ongoing process of how to face something that was denied, a trauma I couldn't cope with. The urge to go to Poland, which came upon me while I was in Paris, was part of my meeting with Europe. Going to Europe, as I express in the first essay, was meant to be something totally different from what I actually discovered. Being in Paris, on the Rue de Rivoli, and seeing that this was a place where World War II actually took place, made that war—which was so far away looking at it from Israel and from our home where my mother's silence blocked it—very real. Suddenly I couldn't run away from it.

JM: So in Paris you began to understand the historical immediacy and continuing trauma of the Occupation and the Holocaust. I suppose, like me, you were shocked to learn about the number of deportations, some 75,000 French Jews—all that history that the French themselves were just starting to deal with.

MG: We never spoke about it in Israel. France was "the seat of the Resistance." We were still very much under the Gaullist myth. But let me place my stories and my first essay against the background of Israeli culture. In Israel, I was a kind of wunderkind, I could have started directing in professional theater before I went to Paris. I was in the right milieu, even for a political career, but I just felt I needed a break. I went to France, with a vague idea of writing about theater and metaphysics. I went in the fall of 72. Nobody could know that the next year would be the Yom Kippur War. We were still in the euphoria of the Six Day War. I recall an image from the last Independence Day before I left for Paris. In Tel Aviv, I saw an army jeep rushing through the city with a flag on top. That image of a military jeep in Tel Aviv, this patriotic image, scared me. I felt it was time to move away, time to go beyond the story in which I'd been raised.

So going to Paris was an opening on many levels. I was breaking away from the expectations and the dominant narrative to look for other things that were hushed up in Israel—the metaphysical, mystical, or religious dimensions of life. At that time I called them "ethical values," and felt that they were hidden under a nationalistic, very hedonistic, materialistic, and atheist mindset. So much happened in that year of arriving in Paris . . . I was looking for something I didn't yet dare name: the Holocaust, the Shoah, which was my mother's story. And, then, the shtetl, what Judaism was before Zionism. Those erased communities and along with them centuries of Jewish life and great achievements in the Diaspora which were seen by Israeli culture a little bit like jokes, or like fictions by Sholem Aleichem. There was no consciousness that all these places had existed such a short time before. And at that time I saw, really saw, for the first time diaspora Jews who lived elsewhere and were not sinners—as they were made to seem by Zionism—sinners because they hadn't left everything on the spot and gone to Israel. This was an inconceivable thing in Israeli sensitivity, because by the fact that they'd stayed in the Diaspora, they'd seemed to put our own existence in question.

JM: You were also coming from a totally different landscape, from the liberated Mediterranean, with its own form of Eros, a secular Sabra, raised in Tel Aviv, with very modern parents. And a resolute determination to be part of the world's modernity.

MG: Yes. And to be cultured. I was eager to absorb art, theater, opera. Yet, with the discovery of European culture many things were hovering, which took me time to recognize. Questions of consciousness and responsibility, and centrally among them was the story of the Holocaust, the question of how it had happened, what had prepared it within this civilization. I see now that I was also coping with my own frightful negation. This has been an ongoing process. But it did start then.

JM: This might be a difficult thing for young readers to grasp because the Shoah, the Holocaust, is anchored in our consciousness now. But it's certainly true that in the early 70s, it wasn't particularly anchored in anybody's consciousness or, rather, people were not talking about it.

MG: Indeed. I think, in fact, that there was an awareness of it in the United States earlier than in Israel. In Israel, the negation went on even longer, hidden under official "commemorations," which were really moments of lip service. But now that the Holocaust is everywhere, there is also a danger of talking too much.

JM: Of making it banal?

MG: Some of the modes of commemoration just reiterate a sadistic urge and draw on the same fascination with violence. They totally ignore what was the real experience, and I mean not only the suffering, but also the facing, the coping with evil inside the ghettoes and the camps, those examples of rare humanity inside the horror. This is an experience that can nourish us, because people still face catastrophes. They still face harsh moral decisions in extreme situations. And if we don't draw lessons from how people cope with them, if we only tell the story of the violence or the suffering, we miss an invaluable lesson about humanity.

JM: I'm thinking about where the Holocaust lives in your stories, especially in "La Promenade." In it we see how survivors filter their experience. So while it's not a story about horror, it's a story about how one lives through horror. We see a kind of heroic survival technique and a yearning for something more—or in the case of one of the characters, a frenzy which keeps him from having to look very deeply. Perhaps part of your mother's story, how she coped or did not cope, and what you saw in her life, had an impact on how you saw those characters and how you wrote that story.

MG: It did. But the story actually came to me in France on two different occasions when I went to seaside towns on the Atlantic Ocean. The first was during my studies, when a bus full of German war veterans filled the streets. This impression was combined with another one I had when I came back to Paris from Israel in the late 1970s and went away for a weekend to Deauville. I remember walking on the promenade by the ocean, and from far away seeing this group of people. They were immediately recognizable—from the way they walked to the way the women held their purses to their hand gestures. It was clear they were not speaking French.

JM: So you saw them as Eastern European Jews, probably Israelis?

MG: Eastern Europeans, not necessarily Israelis. But I felt as though I'd zoomed in to my childhood. And I must confess here that, as I write in the essay "Journey to Poland," going to my Polish Aunt Tonka's was very exotic for me and quite frightening. As a child, I was afraid of the Holocaust survivors that my mother met up with in Tel Aviv. My mode of coping was by being very naughty. Something in these people must have touched me, maybe the tragedy, maybe the pain. My rejection made me cruel! Writing the story obliged me to identify with them, to see from within how such people are sealed away from reality, to listen closely to the way they do and don't express themselves because there was always that silence—to see how memory comes, leaps out constantly, as with the character Lusia, who's not at all my mother. My mother was a very powerful woman.

JM: Yes, your mother was tough.

MG: But at the same time she could subtly change, fall into these reveries. And her face would change completely. As a child, I think I detected those moments because they were the only ones where I really met her, and not just the façade. It was an existential need for me. In that sense maybe Lusia is the incarnation of my mother's inner self, which most of the time she kept under control.

JM: Maybe this inner self was more crucial to her having been able to survive the camps than being the "tough cookie" she presented to the world.

MG: Absolutely. A great Israeli historian, Jacob L.

Talmon, talked to me about survivors when I was directing the J-P Grumberg play about postwar France, *The Workshop*. He said that for many of them if they spoke too much, they wouldn't be able to survive. Not speaking was a way of going on with life. The noisy character in "La Promenade," Hirshel Feingold, is like those Jews wounded by the war who can't stop talking, because the moment they stop all the other voices come back. So Hirshel rushes on, he's successful in business, but he's a kind of mechanized monster—and a victim as well.

JM: In my reading of "La Promenade," I think that Hirshel is the most tragic figure. He's a grotesque clown, a hypercapitalist whom one can't like. But he also sets himself up to be destroyed by his daughter to whom he can only give things.

MG: I know all these characters intimately from my childhood. They haunted me also throughout the writing of my novel, *The Name*. The central character, Amalia, is terribly frightened of them. They embody the unbearable memory from which she keeps running away. But in the end she can see and admit the greatness of what human beings can be beyond their brokenness—even the divinity revealed by the broken soul. Samuel Beckett also helped me understand this.

JM: How so?

MG: The Deauville vision happened right after I finished adapting and directing in Jerusalem a world premier of an early novel of Beckett's, *Mercier and Camier*. The characters resemble Gogo and Didi from *Waiting for Godot*, but instead of just sitting and waiting, they walk without arriving. In my adaptation for the theater, I left the narrator on stage and he followed them on a bicycle. They didn't see him; he saw them. That was a way of placing on stage the presence of several levels of narration.

JM: Which also means many levels of seeing . . .

MG: That enable pathos and empathy beyond the comical and the grotesque. You remember I had to get special permission from Beckett to do this adaptation.

JM: I also remember the description of your meeting with him once you had already directed the play, when you came back to Paris for a visit.

MG: He summoned me, and we had this very long, very moving conversation. He looked closely at the photographs of my show, and while bringing back to mind this early novel he started telling a childhood memory of his strolling with his father in a landscape that inspired the desolate site where the novel ends. I understood then how much Beckett's writing was based on real experience, despite the unreal settings. And then, when I spoke of his own directing of *Waiting for Godot*, he started sketching on a cigarette package the actors' movements on stage. This gave me a rare key to his esthetic and its link to marionette theater. Soon after that, I started writing "La Promenade." The technique of having the narrator speak about the sea as an objective correlative, as Eliot would say, as a way of communicating what goes unsaid inside the characters, was my way of dealing delicately with brokenness, a way of not being too graphic or emotional.

JM: Beckett also uses landscapes and movement to say things without saying them directly.

MG: And to close the circle, Beckett, who for years was seen as a writer of the "Absurd," is to my mind a writer who echoes the Holocaust in an extreme way. His biography reveals his direct links to the events. He survived being denounced as a member of the Resistance, and his friend and first translator to French, Alfred Peron, was tortured to death in Mauthausen while forced to recite poetry, very much like the unforgettable scene with Lucky in *Godot*. But for a long time critics avoided looking at the Shoah's influence on Beckett. I think that's part of the amnesia that shrouded Europe in the 1950s and 60s when Europe was just coming out of the war. I think that, too, was part of a huge cultural repression.

JM: I also think that this "forgetting" might have been absolutely necessary in order for France, and for Europe, to get back on its feet. But you have another similarity with Beckett. He doesn't deal directly with evil. He skirts it. And evil is something you skirt as well.

MG: I think I'm afraid of evil. Although I'm a strong, tall woman, and I have real physical power, when I feel evil directed at me, I totally panic. It's become harder and harder for me to face it, even in writing. Maybe this complicated rapport is also a scar of inherited fear. But I think that in these short stories, in a story like "Between Two and Four," or "The End of the Pythia," I do face evil, or at least portray it in complicated ways.

JM: Very complicated ways. Evil is not monolithic. There's some communication with it. It doesn't appear without an invitation, or at least a hesitant nod in its direction.

MG: You're touching on something here. I don't have a stereotype of "evil," a stock character.

JM: No, you don't have a simplified devil.

MG: Because maybe in a way—and here I am close to Primo Levi, I know there are always grey zones, and that evil also has a human face. Because of that, it's even more frightening. It's always a human potential and until it erupts, you can think that a person is "normal."

Going to Germany for the first time in the 1970s brought this back to me. Who knows how I would have reacted during the War? I recognized that I might have ingredients of evil in myself. I can't reject it as something that is just "out there." And living in the midst of the Middle East conflict requires constant vigilance. I was startled to discover that in the *Kabbalah* Evil is one of God's aspects: "The Other Side." Its existence and the struggle to dominate it by God and Mankind are an ongoing dynamic process.

JM: Your stories are not plot driven, and the questions that you ask are not questions that get answered. Do you think that your experience in Poland, your visit to Auschwitz, your trip to Germany have influenced this kind of open-endedness?

MG: My trip to Poland was part of the coming to writing. It helped me leave behind the certainties, the big ideologies, and listen to what is underneath, enabling me—and I hope my readers—to see that things are not black and white. I think that's part of the ethical mission of writing. To ask questions and to let us know that writing is not a closed world. It emerges from life, and it gives us back to life, maybe with a sharper intuition. How dare we have the hubris of answers?

On style, influences, and technique . . .

JM: I'd like now to ask more specific questions about the stories and about the writing. In this collection there are astonishing changes in register. You go from psychological realism in "La Promenade," to fantastic tales, such as "Hold On to the Sun." You go from ironic description in tales such as "The End of the Pythia" to mystical ecstasy in "Rites of Spring." You also experiment with voicing and levels of consciousness, as in "Jet Lag." There seems to be a real awareness of stylistic experimentation. How were you thinking about the kind of writing you were doing at the time?

MG: Your question brings us back to my literary masters, voices that gave me the feeling that literature was a force in the world, voices like Kafka, Thomas Mann, Rilke, T.S. Eliot, the Hebrew writer Haim Nachman Bialik, who influenced me tremendously, who was a great poet and, at the same time, a wonderful essay and short story writer with a deeply religious background. Through Bialik, I felt the impact of the Jewish book as a continuation of insights through words. Jewish literature turned to fiction very late, only in the nineteenth century. Poetry and prayer were always there, and of course the Bible as text, and an enormous variety of oral genres, later scripted, such as the Talmud or the Midrash. I think there is something in my experimentation in form and in different modes that stems from the shaky ground of what Jewish fiction is. This brought me later to extreme experiments, such as writing *The Making of the Sea: Chronicle of Exegesis* which has the form of a page of the Talmud with a text in the middle and interpretations on the sides. I was also experimenting in the theater, making theater from Jewish ritual. At the same time, I had studied the modernists, and I think that in many ways I *am* a modernist.

And modernism is an experimentation of what the mind is and how we express the mind through language. Today I find incredible resonances between my search for a poetics and research in neuroscience! I experiment, for example, with what I call organic writing, something that reverberates in the body of the reader, how through jumps of consciousness enacted in the mind of the reader the reader becomes an actor who performs the text. Like the neuroscientist, the writer with her art forges the tools to make the mind readable, to shape it. My older daughter is now researching the way autistic children draw on preconceived narratives in order to construct their own self. We all, to a certain extent, do that.

JM: And if we can change the narratives, there's the potential to change the self.

MG: Yes, we can transform our life narratives, get free from plots that trap us, open new ways to tell ourselves what is good or bad. That is what a successful psychoanalysis offers—the replacement of a narrative, or a new perspective on it. We cannot live without narratives, and tradition means their transmission. Yet narratives have to be constantly questioned—both ideologies and religious narratives—that's our role and task as individuals faced with a constantly changing world.

JM: In working with these translations, I read and reread your texts and I was struck by a certain coherency, despite the formal experimentation. The first aspect of this coherency, which we've already hinted at in talking about "La Promenade," is an extreme sensitivity to light, to the movement of light, and therefore to darkness, to variations on what one can see as fundamental to setting the mood and to suggesting a character's reality. Why do you work so much with light?

MG: Maybe because of my first important memory, which came back again recently when I started to write about my mother. She would come into my childhood room which faced the east. The shutters would still be closed, but through the blinds came a shaft of light, full of these little hovering particles of dust. She would point and say, "Sweetheart, this is light." I would be totally carried away to somewhere beyond the closed shutters and the room. This penetration by that other place impregnated me with a deep sense of what light is. It's at the core of my writing. It's in the psyche of the characters and in the narrating voice. It is amazement.

JM: Amazement is basic to all of your stories.

MG: For me, it's almost a synonym for the writing mode. Amazement crosses your routine and it stops you. In my novel *Snapshots* I even use an "amazement technique." You're on the New Jersey turnpike, and suddenly some totally industrial piece of landscape evokes an emotion and you're reminded of something else and you're split open. These moments of synesthesia, when the senses all mesh together, heighten your perception and bring us close to ecstasy, to a mystical experience.

JM: In order to have the necessary tension and excitement for a viable short story, you create very vibrant characters. They may have moments where they dim, but they are really very alive, awash in desire.

MG: Something that runs through all my stories is a longing, conscious or unconscious, for those brief revelations of daily life. These are the blessed moments, which can occur outside of any religion or organized belief. They are moments of intense life, of intense memory, pain, yearning, moments of sudden epiphany. They have fascinated me always and they echo closely Hasidic theology, which has a pantheistic thrust. You can find God in a blade of grass. It echoes also that quote from Nicolas Malebranche speaking about Kafka that was quoted by Walter Benjamin and finally by Paul Celan: "Attention is the silent prayer of the soul."

JM: But at the same time that there's this great attention and this constant revelation of surrounding life, there's also in all your stories a sense of movement. The characters, but also the landscapes, are almost never still, even when they try to be so. They sway, they teeter, they totter—and you know the difficulties we had trying to find the right verbs in English for the verbs in Hebrew that communicate all these motions. But the movement that grabs me in your stories is the inner turmoil, the inability to rest, the electric quality of nature and human beings constantly striving, transforming, never at peace.

MG: "La Promenade"—its ironic title drawn from the name of the fictional café—has that connotation of movement to it, of people who keep on keeping on, who go on being those who are placeless or have been . . .

JM: Exiled. Aren't we back to the notion of the wanderer?

MG: Of the wanderer. Of the exiled. I think that's something I wasn't consciously aware of. That's part of the unconscious level of writing. But I think now that it's also part of my exiting from a certain Israeli culture that pretended: "We've finally arrived. We're at The Place." By uprooting my characters from this certainty of place, they begin to long to be part of a landscape.

JM: And they long for different stories, but also for a place of plenitude and peace.

MG: I think that is what I sensed and sense even today about Israeli culture, that (to paraphrase a metaphor of the great poet Yehuda Amichai) the liquid is still shaking in the vessels, vessels which had been uprooted and re-rooted but were still shaking, still being formed.

JM: This also goes back to writing through the body, and wanting to make fictional bodies resonate and reverberate in the minds and the bodies of the readers. Because you are also a very physical writer. Your characters are walking, or they're riding bikes; they're traveling in a plane; they're dancing, or they're capering foolishly.

MG: Experiencing through the body is something very central for me. I don't know if it has to do with being a woman writer. But I feel the need to locate the mind in a way that the body not only expresses it, but even foresees it—as if when you do something it has already been enacted unconsciously in parts of your being that are considered less "intelligent." You've experienced the rush of the blood, the perspiration, the heart pangs, and then the thought comes out. Zooming into this dark zone for a fraction of a second always attracted me as revelatory of the impulses that set in motion how we act and how we react.

JM: Your experience as a theater person, and your appreciation of the stories you physically performed at the Lecoq school when you were in Paris have no doubt reinforced this centrality of the body. In theater, for an actor to put forth the truth of a human being, it has to be through the body.

MG: True. And just like not starting a rehearsal without a physical warm-up, I won't start a morning of writing without warming up, because I know I write from the body as well. And from theater I know that personal expression comes mainly from body movement, body language, and not from what you say.

JM: Can we talk about the place of the uncanny in your work? While we've arranged your stories according to their degree of departure from the conventions of realism, there are obvious portents and magical signs in even some of the more realistic portraits. In "Elijah's Sabbath Days," for example, there are dreamscapes that tell us other truths, contradictory, troubling truths. I'm wondering to what extent these different levels of possibility, these ways of making animate what is normally inanimate, are projections against the incursion of death, which is, of course, how Freud postulates the uncanny.

MG: I don't think I've experienced these stories as facing death. I would even say I don't feel I've dared touch this subject in my writing in a direct way until very recently. Maybe rather than death and the uncanny, there is in my stories a realm of being that's different from what is usually connoted as "being." The character Berenov and the people of the island in "Rites of Spring" experience death as a mystical moment of bliss. Maybe that's a way of running away from death . . .

JM: Or maybe it's a different way of understanding death.

MG: Or aspiring to something else. I think what you call "uncanny" was my way of dealing with the beyond. With what is beyond material reality.

JM: Perhaps the uncanny is the wrong term. But there is a fantastical weirdness in your character Berenov turning into a tree, for example, in his becoming living vegetation.

MG: That was, I suspect, my way of coping with old age. I wrote that when my father started to grow old. I think I was working through the decaying of the body, and the freedom of the emotions, of the soul, in a decaying body. Berenov permits himself to succumb to something that was always there, like a call—and he blooms in a certain way. A sudden bloom because he gives in to an inner urge that he'd been repressing all those years. In Hasidic thought there is this moment of ecstasy when the soul leaves the body to cleave with that which is beyond it. It can occur in the moment you say, "Hear, Oh Israel." I was very much immersed at the time of writing "Rites of Spring" in that way of Hassidic thinking. I could see these moments of disappearance as a reversal into something extremely positive. Let me tell you the anecdote of sending "Rites of Spring" from Paris to Tel Aviv. I was terrified by how my parents were going to read it, and what they were going to think about their daughter, whom they had sent to do her PhD in Paris, sending them back this strange story about a man who gropes about in the toilet and . . .

JM: And reaches for the key that he's lost down the drain and ends up with a handful of shit.

MG: Yes. So what were they going to think about me? To my amazement and gratitude, I got back a typed text from my father——because a handwritten manuscript wouldn't have been good enough. He actually sent me the first review I ever had——and in it he interprets that moment of Berenov touching the shit in a traditional Hasidic way.

JM: He was raised in a Hasidic environment? I only knew how much of an active Socialist and even a secularist he was.

MG: There's a direct line from the Hasidic legacy to the Zionist pioneers. This is still largely ignored by the official narrative, and I discovered it vividly while working on my father's and grandfather's memoirs. Our family was unusual, as four generations arrived in the 20s, from the pious great-grandfather to the socialist secular grandsons. There wasn't a break between the generations. They shared the same Zionist dream even if articulated in different forms. I have memories of my father dancing Hasidic dances, joking in Yiddish, singing Hasidic songs with his brother who was a member of the Knesset and a minister of the Labor Party. My father embodied this energy is his world vision very powerfully. So in his "review" he writes to me: "Berenov touches the manure and that's how we know he's alive!" And I realized that my father understood my story in a way I didn't dare see it, as the Hasidic gesture of descending far below for the sake of rising upwards.

On writing and politics . . .

JM: I've heard you worry about the overt secularism of contemporary Israeli literature. I wonder, then, if you write in part to create a balance in Israeli fiction. For, as we've discussed, there's this mystical yearning and belief in much of what you write.

MG: I realize now that I began to write also as a rebellious act, rebelling against the generation before me, the generation of Amos Oz and A.B. Yehoshua, all those major realist male writers. I always felt closer to Bialik, as I've mentioned before, to Shmuel Yossef Agnon, to Aharon Appelfeld's lyrical prose. In that sense I was overtly rebelling against the dominant tradition of what Israeli literature is or "should be," in which the writer, also an intellectual, is meant to form a kind of collective ideological identity or "Israelness," as if there were such a monolithic thing.

JM: You've talked both about the necessity of mythic structures created through narrative and also about their pervasive danger.

MG: I do think that what's going on in the conflict in the Middle East is in large part a war between the three monotheistic narratives, Judaism, Christianity, and Islam. Stories can enclose one community and pit it against the other. The battles among these three religions are all mythical wars that have in them questions of exclusivity, of who is right, who is wrong. And these myths go very deep. Anti-Semitism is a good example of the damages stories can inflict. I even think we can tie misogynistic myths to anti-Semitism. Jews have often been seen as "effeminate" or even as "sinful women." With the legacy of Zionism on one side of my family and of the Holocaust from my mother's side—which results from a national narrative that brought Germany to a state of madness—I was always conscious both of the ideological dimension of stories and of the unstoppable process of story-making. I think that is why as a writer I turned to a "reality" that carries layers we do not see. This mythic dimension is inherent to traditional Jewish writing that always has traces of the presence (or the deplored absence) of God. Later, I understood that more than being a Jewish writer, I was and am a Jewish *woman* writer.

JM: You've written elsewhere about the image and status of women in Jewish myth and literature and about the imbrication of global feminism and Jewish womanhood. Here is a passage from your essay, "The Jewish Literary Manifesto, First Person Feminine": "The power of anarchy, of 'to the contrary,' characterizes the woman's voice in Jewish myth. It displaces ruling authorities or fossilized truths, thereby awaking rage or mockery. Nevertheless, through the slyness of comedy, the power of passion and Eros, or the strength of remonstration, it can succeed in overturning even God's plans. The change in women's status in global society is generating an unprecedented revolution in the place of women in Jewish culture, in a time when Jewish history veers between the poles of destruction and renewal." You imply some key questions and suggest some potentially stunning changes in the status of women in this passage. And yet I've never thought of you as a militant writer for women's rights.

MG: No, I'm not. In my childhood and adolescence, as I was the only child of a late second marriage, I was the tomboy. I was the strongest "guy" in the neighborhood, retrieving items that fell out of windows and into the trees for the neighbors. But as I grew older, I began to listen to all the other voices that came through my body. I now think that containing all of them is a feminine way of listening. For if a mother weren't able to love all her children, and be able to contain their oppositions, how would we live? It's true I never adhered to any feminist . . .

JM: Movement. No, I know.

MG: But I do claim in my lonely way another path. Another path to what womanhood might be: On the one hand the power of holding a total reality, as Emmanuel Levinas might put it. On the other, eclipsing myself, creating the place for all my "children," in whatever form they take, to be what they are, to be amazed by the richness they bring back to me, a richness that the mother's embrace enables. Being in control and creating a space where things can happen; letting others be without immediately controlling them. For me that is a feminine or a woman's way of being, of giving life.

On the work of translation . . .

JM: I'd like to turn to the question of translation because for days now we've been reading your work aloud in English and fussing, fumbling, struggling to edit the translations and get the English just right, or as right as possible, but also to capture the multiple layers in your texts.

MG: I'm so glad for this chance to revisit the English and to strive towards a harmonizing of the voices given to me by other translators, especially because I'm more and more confident of what I should sound like in English.

JM: And I'm sure translators like Barbara Harshav, Dalya Bilu, and Peter Cole have helped build this confidence. But what haven't we been able to do because of the difficulty of moving from Hebrew to English?

MG: Hebrew is an extraordinary literary language, and with Chinese the only language that has carried history in an uninterrupted way from Antiquity to the present. Hebrew contains the Bible and the ancient Dead Sea Scrolls, all the layers of the Talmud, the mystical writings of the Middle Ages, Maimonides, Enlightenment literature, modern poetry, street slang. All of them can be contained in one piece, and they can live next to each other. It's an extraordinarily rich tool, very intertextual.

With Hebrew, when you use a word tied to a special context in another context it immediately sets up a reverberation. A Hebrew-speaking reader will experience a kind of doubling of references. You remember that we were looking for . . .

JM: A way in English to make proper names, such as Hila (which means "light") from "Elijah's Sabbath Days" or Nammi (which means "the sleeper") from "Jet Lag" keep their second symbolic meaning. And how we searched for an English word that could mean "wind" and "spirit" as one

Hebrew word does. But there wasn't a way to capture this particular polyvalency.

MG: And in "Hold On to the Sun" I also employed the kind of Hebrew used in early translations of American English. So there were all these layers of language we had to attack. Sometimes coming back to modern English to find the words was great and other times we had to use a King James type of English. The King James quality gives a mythic feel to some of the texts' language—a feeling of heightened oratory. But I must say that while some things are lost in translation, I'm not less intrigued by what is gained.

JM: And what *is* gained?

MG: Translation happens in every act of reading. That's why I see my readers as intimate collaborators. The writing lives only once it's read, and it's always read in a different way by whatever mind it crosses. The closest experience of knowing what's going on in the mind of a reader is when you have to interpret your text in another language and you say overtly: "We're translating." You see how the piece of writing is not yours anymore. It's again the gesture of a mother: You let the child go; you don't possess it; you don't own it. It's not "yours," and it lives another life. Language is always beyond the individual writer, the individual mind. Walter Benjamin calls it "pure language."

JM: I'm glad to hear this because you know there were many moments when I was quite frustrated while we revised the translations worrying about the particularities of English verbs impoverishing the ambiance created through the Hebrew.

MG: It was a very special experience of translating and editing. You, not speaking Hebrew, had to recreate in your mind a seasoned, chiseled linguistic reality—without bumps and bizarre moments. Your experience in translating from the French, the way you've shared my writing, and our past collaboration in the theater were reassuring and fascinating to me. You pull the translation totally into an English landscape, knowing that my writing comes from somewhere else and wanting that somewhere else to be acknowledged.

JM: Yes. I don't think what we've done is to evacuate the Hebrew and make the stories so colloquially American or so specifically American that they couldn't be coming from another culture or another language. That possible otherness is easier to find with your stories because they do have a legendary aspect; they are highly stylized and one can't really flatten them. But my biggest anxiety, as it would have been for anyone who translates literature, was how to capture the degree of "particularness" and of exploration in your original language. You push and pull Hebrew to make it do things that other writers don't do. I worried about finding similar ways of pushing English without making it sound overly precious.

MG: I think some of the moments of collaboration were like writing together, because we were experimenting with the possible order of words, how to enter a sentence so the reader experiences what the character experiences at the same time. I really appreciated the fierceness of our linguistic debates.

On exile, the limits of framing, eroticism, and allegory . . .

JM: Why does the Pythia, that golem-like avenger, turn up in your writing?

MG: "The End of the Pythia" came upon me while I was trying to observe the Sabbath in Paris while living in that garret on the Rue de Rivoli, on the most crowded shopping day on a street known for its shops. I remember once needing to buy a can opener. I went through all these alleys of things in the basement of the biggest department store in Paris. I was in this temple of cutlery; there were hundreds of kinds of can openers. I began to tremble, seeing how much you can have and how little you need, seeing the homeless, seeing Europe and the power of culture, and was shocked feeling that despite this refinement many horrors happened there, and nothing stopped while they went on. The story begins with a nod to Bialik's prose poem, "The Scroll of Fire," which is about the destruction of the Temple and the exile of the Divine Presence from its ruins. The cadence of Bialik's sentences launches the "Pythia," a legend about destruction and exile and the world in chaos.

JM: There's also a supermarket aspect to this world, a story of life as consumerism.

MG: Life as piles. Piles of suitcases, piles of purses, piles of glasses, just like at Auschwitz, as I later understood.

JM: What an image! Speaking of images—by dint of what they do, some of your characters function as framing eyes—the photographer in "Hold On to the Sun," for instance. These characters catch reality through long descriptions.

MG: That's an intuition of the way we conceive of the world as images. Think about how we live more and more in a visual world, how often people tell their lives through Facebook, through posting pictures, through You Tube. We see reality as if it were a photograph, a movie, a television show that we orchestrate ourselves. And the world of literature, this old mode of words, has the power to decompose or to deconstruct this way of looking and to look behind and beyond.

JM: What you're showing us, in fact, is the inadequacy of this kind of framing to capture everything that's real. And among what's real, there's eroticism, very present in your stories and never resulting in what we could call "a love story." There's a longing for coupling, a move toward a possible, licit couple—in the case of the characters Elijah and Hila in "Elijah's Sabbath Days." But there's also violation through desire—in the child molestation of "From Two to Four." In "Jet Lag" the main character sees the potential of desire but gets lost in a time warp. Yet having experienced desire his life will never be the same—or his wife's either. Somehow she's really lost out. These are anxious stories for me: Eros and violation exist side by side.

MG: Eros has a very central part in my writing. It's clearly one of the mysteries of life that I explore, another form of revelation. I think that Eros reveals libido, the power of life. I know, for example, that I can attribute my mother's survival to libido. Her desire to "be a woman," to have children, to raise them, to live in her body was something transferred to me.

JM: In your stories Eros is not necessarily coded "good" or "evil," which means Eros can also be distressing. In "From Two to Four" there's no condemnation of the violator or the potential violator. In a certain form of feminist writing, and in a certain phase of feminist writing, these violators would have been set up to be crucified.

MG: Maybe my lack of overt condemnation shows us the complexities of things we must try to understand. Eros is a major factor of life and it has a very contradictory set of manifestations. We tend to be afraid of these contradictions and shun them because they're not something you can enact. You sublimate them. But in literature you can express the urge that precedes the sublimation.

JM: Maybe it's also about guilt feelings and the chance to express them as well.

MG: In "Between Two and Four" what interests me are

the stages of desire's awakening, when it emerges from the body at a very young age, before the mind is ready. The girl is aware of the gardener but she doesn't know how to decipher his look. She has erotic urges that are totally innocent, that are part of childhood. To deny their existence would be mutilating. The abusing of this innocence, as the gardener does, is a betrayal of adult responsibility. But we cannot forget that to hurt, to do ill is also driven by an erotic urge. My obsession with trying to understand Eros is also an oblique way of getting to the riddle of sadism, of why people torture other people. Beyond all the historical, economic, ideological explanations, there's that person to person relationship, something that happens in the psyche that connects body to body. And there are more and more torturers in this world.

JM: May I close by bringing up the question of allegory and the kind of allegorical tales included in this collection, especially "Rites of Spring" and "Hold On to the Sun."

MG: Rabbi Nachman of Bratslav, who inspired the theater piece we did in Paris in 1974, used to say "Better teach through stories than through lectures," because a story can capture secrets through the possibility of contradictions, through speaking about good and evil as they're combined in the world. The legends in this collection (or allegorical tales as you call them) are not really lessons but rather ways of coming to terms with the world. The rage against God that I inherited from my mother infuses them, as do a longing and yearning for His eternal presence. Yet He hides.

JM: God is under the mist, in the dimness, or in the fog. And in the nightfall that also constitutes so much of this writing of yours.

MG: But in "Hold On to the Sun," he's also there in the fantastic hope that undergirds everyone's quest—to stop time, to realize eternity.

JM: The photographer and the young woman in this story both die and don't achieve their heart's desire. And the scholar is so obsessive that he never really has a life.

MG: But he has his learning.

JM: Yes, but the scholar's staying with the books, secluded, is not a hopeful option for me.

MG: I think we differ in the way we read this story and that has to do, I believe, with the different deep narratives we react to.

JM: Maybe that's where it shows that your backgound is Jewish and that I was schooled by Unitarians!

MG: Probably. And so we attribute a different place to "learning," especially as being part of Eros.

JM: Traditionally, of course, for men it was.

MG: The Eros of learning is part of a Jewish man's life. So, in the story the scholar's dedication to his research is a replacement for love. His outrageous hope of eternal light is the most daringly erotic experience of his whole life.

JM: But the story also treats the scholar in quite an ironic way.

MG: Yes, and on several levels. This man, whose hope is profoundly mystical, lives a secular life. It was characteristic of the Jerusalem I could still find on my return to Israel in the late 1970s. One could meet in the street great scholars, like Gershom Scholem or Haim Schirman, scholars who dedicated their lives to study, living secular, childless, or lonely lives. It was a generation of great European minds expelled from Europe, but also cut off from the old world of the shtetl where they didn't belong anymore. The old orthodox neighborhoods of Jerusalem kept the secret of this vanished world yet they were zones of unreachable desire.

JM: Quite unreachable for the scholar in the story . . .

MG: Nevertheless, the traces of hope, the memory of redemption, lived on. . . . I think this is what I meant by calling the anthology *Hold On to the Sun*. I claimed the power to seek the traces of the dismissed voices of tradition, to create a fuller identity for Israelis, perhaps even to inscribe new marks.

ACKNOWLEDGMENTS

The writing of a book encounters those readers who as sounding boards bring it into being—even more so in the burgeoning first years of literary writing.

My parents, Rina and Pinchas Govrin, profoundly conversant with world literature and the treasures of Hebrew, were my first addressees. Michaël and Emmanuel Levinas, Emmanuel and Stéphan Mosès, Uri and Shlomo Pinès, Shlomith Rimmon-Kenan, David Brezis, and Jacques Derrida later joined them. They read what was exposed and what was concealed between the lines, and they heard the continuing voice from the Jewish mystical tradition to modern avant-garde prose.

Parts of these stories were written all over the world during my travels with Haim Brezis, my companion and husband. Those were still the days of the typewriter, and in order to minimize its sound I used to leave our room to type on whatever shore was nearby. These landscapes, including the childhood northern seascape of Becki Brezis, my mother-in-law, reverberate in the writing.

My thanks to Menachem Peri and Moshe Ron, the editors of the original Hebrew text, *Hold On to the Sun: Short Stories and Legends*. Thanks also to David Rosenberg, whose enthusiasm as an ever close reader resulted in the commission of the first English translation. Thanks, too, to Nili Cohen and The Institute for the Translation of Hebrew Literature for their support and to Dalya Bilu for the original careful translation into English. My friends Irène Shraer and Nessa Rapoport spontaneously translated their own readings into French and English which encouraged me to think internationally. The Jerusalem poets' friendship with Peter Cole brought about the joint translation of the poem "Won't You See" that opens the book.

Gila Ramras-Rauch included "La Promenade," then published in a magazine, in her anthology, *Facing the Holocaust*, and Leo Edelstein, the editor of *Pataphysics* (whom I met in Melbourne thanks to David Shapiro and the international "poetry network"), first published the story "Hold On to the Sun." In my last overseas telephone conversation with Shaindy Rudoff, before her premature death, she asked for "Between Two and Four" for *Maggid*'s issue on "Jewish Bodies," edited by Michael Kramer.

The essays, written along the years, are part of my

ongoing conversation with my mother—during her life and after her death. In publishing this book, I hope to honor all those people who generously transmitted to me bits and pieces of her story.

I am grateful to Rachel Feldhay Brenner and to Alan Berger, the editor of *Second Generation Voices,* thanks to whom I added the meditation "Journey to Poland" to the original "Letter from the Regions of Delusion," addressed to my parents. The original letter was published by Yzhak Bezalel in *Davar*, and years later Yaakov Besser published the full two-part essay in *Itton 77*. Barbara Harshav hears deeply my voice in her translations both of my novels and of two of the essays included here. William Philips and Edith Kurzweil opened to me for years the *Partisan Review* as another "home for thinking." I am grateful to all of them. "Facing Evil" was written at the request of Noah Flug, the president of the International Auschwitz Committee, and originally published in *Ha'aretz*. I'm grateful to Ilana Kurshan for reviewing its translation. Basmat Hazan encouraged me to write "*Selichot* in Krakow: Migrations of a Melody," and Adam Rovner published it in the online journal *Zeek*— along with a fragment of my mother's recorded voice.

As always, my gratitude goes to Deborah Harris, my agent and friend. But it is Judith Graves Miller who is responsible for the present iteration of *Hold On to the Sun: True Stories and Tales,* from its conception to her sensitive and uncompromising revision of the translations. I want to thank her for the immense pleasure of collaboration, but not less for our many years of literary, theatrical, and personal friendship that stand as proof of art's power to cross languages and cultures.

Author and editor give their warmest thanks and affection to the exemplary staff at the Feminist Press, to executive director Gloria Jacobs, and to Elaine Reuben and Shulamit Reinharz of the Reuben/Rifkin Jewish Women Writers Series for encouraging and finally bringing to fruition this collection of texts. Working together has been joyful as well as professionally gratifying.

Judith G. Miller extends her thanks to New York University for its support of her research and to The Department of French, especially to Ellie Vance and to Elizabeth Applegate, for clerical and other help with this project. She would like most especially to thank Michal Govrin for the opportunity of making *Hold On to the Sun* appear with the Feminist Press, and for her steadfast love and the extraordinary stimulation of our conversations over thirty years of life.

CREDITS

The short stories in this collection were originally published in Hebrew in Le'echoz Ba'shemesh, Sipurim Ve'agadot (*Hold On to the Sun: Short Stories and Legends*) by Michal Govrin, Siman Kria/HaKibbutz HaMeuchad, 1984. The original English translation was provided by The Institute for the Translation of Hebrew Literature. The original translation was revised by Judith G. Miller and Michal Govrin.

Aharon Appelfeld's quote was translated from the Hebrew by Gabriel Levin.

The poem "Won't You See" was originally published in Hebrew in Ota Sha'a (*That Very Hour*) by Michal Govrin, Sifirat Poalim, 1981. It was translated from the Hebrew by the author, with Peter Cole.

273

The essay "Journey to Poland" was translated from the Hebrew by Barbara Harshav.

The short story "La Promenade: Triptych," parts I, II, and III were originally translated from the Hebrew by Dalya Bilu.

The short story "Between Two and Four" was originally translated from the Hebrew by Dalya Bilu and revised by Michael P. Kramer.

The short story "Elijah's Sabbath Days" was originally translated from the Hebrew by Dalya Bilu.

The short story "Evening Ride" was originally translated from the Hebrew by Dalya Bilu.

The short story "Jet Lag" was originally translated from the Hebrew by Dalya Bilu.

The short story "The End of Pythia" was originally translated from the Hebrew by Dalya Bilu.

The short story "The Dance of the Thinker" was originally translated from the Hebrew by Dalya Bilu.

The short story "Rites of Spring" was originally translated from the Hebrew by Dayla Bilu.

The short story "Hold On to the Sun" was originally translated from the Hebrew by Dayla Bilu.

The essay "Facing Evil: Thoughts on a Visit to Auschwitz" was translated from the Hebrew by Barbara Harshav.

The essay "*Selichot* in Krakow: Migrations of a Melody" was translated from the Hebrew by Anat Schultz, edited by Adam Rovner, with Yiddish transliteration by Adam Rubin.

We hope you enjoyed this book.

Without support from our readers, we can't publish books like *Hold On to the Sun*, which need to be out in the world, reminding us of all the untold stories. If you like what we are doing, please consider making a donation to the Feminist Press. No amount is too small. Please visit our website, **feministpress.org**, to make a donation online, or join the Friends of FP to receive all our books at a great discount. You can also send a check directly to the Feminist Press at CUNY, 365 Fifth Avenue, Suite 5406, New York, NY 10016. Thank you for reading, and for making these books possible.

■

The Feminist Press is an independent nonprofit literary publisher that promotes freedom of expression and social justice. We publish exciting writing by women and men who share an activist spirit and a belief in choice and equality. Founded in 1970, we began by rescuing "lost" works by writers such as Zora Neale Hurston and Charlotte Perkins Gilman, and established our publishing program with books by American writers of diverse racial and class backgrounds. Since then we have also been bringing works from around the world to North American readers. We seek out innovative, often surprising books that tell a different story.

See our complete list of books at **feministpress.org**.

THE FEMINIST PRESS
AT THE CITY UNIVERSITY OF NEW YORK
FEMINISTPRESS.ORG